ALSO BY CALVIN TRILLIN

TEPPER ISN'T GOING OUT

CALVIN TRILLIN

Tepper Isn't Going Out

a novel

RANDOM HOUSE NEW YORK

Copyright © 2001 by Calvin Trillin

All rights reserved under International and Pan-American Copyright
Conventions. Published in the United States by Random House, Inc.,
New York, and simultaneously in Canada by Random House
of Canada Limited, Toronto.

RANDOM HOUSE and colophon are registered
trademarks of Random House, Inc.

A version of this book's opening scene appeared as
a short story in *The New Yorker.*

Library of Congress Cataloging-in-Publication Data

Trillin, Calvin.
Tepper isn't going out : a novel/Calvin Trillin.
p. cm.
ISBN 0-375-50676-4
1. Eccentrics and eccentricities—Fiction. 2. Automobile parking—
Fiction. 3. New York (N.Y.)—Fiction. 4. Celebrities—Fiction. I. Title.
PS3570.R5 T4 2002
813'.54—dc21   2001031863

Printed in the United States of America on acid-free paper
Random House website address: www.atrandom.com

2 4 6 8 9 7 5 3

FIRST EDITION

Book design by Barbara M. Bachman

I wrote this for Alice. Actually,
I wrote everything for Alice.

TEPPER ISN'T GOING OUT

1. *Curtain Time*

"IT'S ABSOLUTELY UNCONSCIONABLE," THE YOUNG MAN said loudly, shaking a banana in front of the fruit peddler's face. "It's simply not to be believed. It's unbelievable."

Murray Tepper looked up from his newspaper to see what was happening. Tepper was sitting behind the wheel of a dark blue Chevrolet Malibu that was parked on the uptown side of Forty-third Street, between Fifth and Sixth. Across the street, an argument was going on between an intense young man in a suit and the peddler who set up a stand on Forty-third Street every day to sell apples and bananas and peaches to office workers. Tepper had seen them go at it before. The young man was complaining about the price that the peddler charged for a single banana. The peddler was defending himself in an accent that Tepper couldn't place even by continent. There had been a time when the accents of New York fruit peddlers were dependably Italian—Tepper had for years thought of "banana" as a more or less Italian word, in the way that some New Yorkers thought of "aggravation" as a more or less Yiddish word—but that time had long passed. As the young man in the suit practically pulsated with outrage, the peddler repeated a single phrase over and over again in his mysterious accent. Finally, Tepper was able to figure out what the peddler kept saying: "free-market economy, free-market economy, free-market economy. . . ."

It was six-thirty on a Tuesday evening in May, at the tag end of the second millennium. The air was mild. For ten days, there had been clear skies and spring temperatures, disappointing those New Yorkers who liked to complain every May that the weather had changed from bitterly cold winter to brutally hot summer as if God—a stern and vengeful God—had flipped a switch. Tepper was comfortable in the suit he'd worn to work that day—a garment that was in the category he sometimes referred to as "office suits," slightly worn and maybe a bit shiny at the elbows. He thought of his office suits as the equivalents of the suits a high-school teacher nearing retirement age might wear to school. In fact, Tepper thought of himself as looking a bit like a high-school teacher nearing retirement age—a medium-sized man with thin hair going gray and a face that didn't seem designed to hold an expression long.

There was plenty of light left on Forty-third Street. Tepper was reading the *New York Post*, which he still considered an evening paper, even though it had been coming out in the morning for years. The proprietors of the *Post* could publish it any time of day they wanted to; Tepper read it in the evening. People who had finished up late at the office were walking briskly toward the subway stops or Grand Central. A few of them, before going their separate ways, stopped to chat with colleagues at building entrances. The chats tended to be brief, perhaps because the entrances still smelled something like the bottom of an ashtray from a full day of smokers having ducked out of their smoke-free offices to pace up and down in front of the building, taking long, purposeful drags and exchanging nods now and then, like lifers in the exercise yard greeting people to whom they had long ago said everything they had to say.

Aside from an occasional argument over the price of fruit, Forty-third Street didn't provide much entertainment for Tepper. Forty-seventh Street between Fifth and Sixth, just a few blocks uptown, would undoubtedly be livelier. Forty-seventh Street was the diamond district, after all, and it had always fielded an interesting variety of pedestrians—Hasidic Jews taking a break from their diamond-cutting jobs, young couples on their way to buy an engagement ring from a dealer who had apparently given a very good deal to some acquaintance's brother-in-law's uncle, innocuous-looking security people on the alert for thieves who knew that any number of people walked up and down Forty-seventh Street with thousands of dollars' worth of diamonds jangling in their pockets. Tepper had, in fact, bought his wife's engagement ring on Forty-seventh Street many years before, from a man whose device for building trust was to confide in the customer about the perfidy of other dealers.

"See that one over there," Tepper's dealer had said, indicating with a quick jerk of his eyebrows a small man in the booth across the way. "Perlmutter. I saw him sell a piece of cut glass to a young couple by implying, without actually saying so in so many words, that it was a four-carat diamond that may have been—*may* have been, he wanted to emphasize; he didn't claim to have proof of this—worn by Marie of Rumania. The boy he was talking to was a yokel, a farmer. You could practically see the hay coming out of his ears. He looked like he came from Indiana or Idaho or one of them. Perlmutter had to spell 'Rumania' for him. Maybe 'Marie,'

5

too; I don't remember. The yokel bought the ring. A *shonda* was what that was, young man. A scandal. A disgrace to the trade and to those of us trying to make an honest living. Now, let me show you a small but elegant little stone that, to be quite frank with you . . ."

Forty-seventh Street would be livelier, Tepper thought, although the dealer who'd pointed out the wily Perlmutter was undoubtedly long gone and these days a lot of young couples probably bought their engagement rings over the Internet.

Behind Tepper, a car was coming slowly down Forty-third Street. As it passed the imposing structure occupied by the Century Club, it slowed even more, and, a few yards farther, came to a stop just behind Tepper's Chevrolet. Taking his eyes away from the paper for only an instant, Tepper shot a quick glance toward his side mirror. He could see a Mercury with New Jersey license plates—probably theatergoers from the suburbs who knew that these streets in the forties were legal for long-term metered parking after six. The New Jersey people would be hoping to find a spot, grab a bite in a sushi bar or a deli, and then walk to the theater. Good planners, people from New Jersey, Tepper thought, except for the plan they must have hatched at some point to move to New Jersey. (The possibility that anybody started out in New Jersey—that any number of people had actually been born there—was not a possibility Tepper had ever dwelled on.) He pretended to concentrate on his newspaper, although he was, in fact, still thinking of the state of New Jersey, which he envisioned as a series of vast shopping-mall parking lots, where any fool could find a spot. The Mercury's driver tapped his horn a couple of times, and then, getting no response, moved even with Tepper's Chevy. The woman who was sitting on the passenger side stuck her head out of the window and said, "Going out?"

Tepper said nothing.

"Are you going out?" the woman asked again.

Tepper did not look up, but with his right hand he reached over toward the window and wagged his index finger back and forth, in the gesture some Southern Europeans have perfected as a way of dealing with solicitations from shoeshine boys or beggars. Tepper had been able to wag his finger in the negative with some authority since 1954, when, as a young draftee who regularly reminded himself to be grateful that at least the shooting had stopped, he spent thirteen miserable months as a clerk-typist in a motor pool in Pusan and had to ward off prostitutes and beggars every time he left the base. An acquaintance had once expressed envy for the gesture as something that seemed quite cosmopolitan, but Tepper would have traded it in an instant for the ability to do the legendary New York taxi-hailing whistle that was accomplished by jamming a finger in each corner of the mouth.

He had never been able to master that whistle, despite years of patient coaching by a doorman named Hector, on West Eighty-third. Tepper had encountered Hector while looking for overnight parking spots in his own neighborhood, in the days before his wife managed to persuade him to take space for his car by the month in a multilevel garage a few blocks from their apartment. He hadn't seen anybody use the fingers-in-the-mouth whistle on the street for a long time. He hadn't tried it for a long time himself. Was it something that might simply come to him, after all these years? Now that he wasn't trying it several evenings a week under the pressure of Hector's watchful eye, might it just appear, the way a smooth golf swing sometimes comes inexplicably to duffers once the tension of their expensive lessons has ended? He was about to jam a couple of fingers in the corners of his mouth to see if the gift might have arrived unannounced when he realized that the Mercury was still idling next to him, making it necessary to remain focused on the newspaper.

"He's not going out," the woman shouted to the man at the wheel, loudly enough for Tepper to hear.

"He's not going out?" the driver shouted back, sounding incredulous. "What do you mean he's not going out?"

"He probably parks there just before six and sits there so he can tell people he's not going out," the woman shouted.

The driver gunned the motor in irritation, and the Mercury from New Jersey pulled away. Just past the entrance to the Princeton Club, it briefly stopped again, the occupants apparently having mistaken a no-parking zone in front of the post office for a legal spot. Then the driver slowly made his way toward Sixth Avenue, speeding up suddenly when a spot came open on the left and screeching to a halt a moment later as a sport-utility vehicle two cars in front of him positioned itself to go into the spot. The woman got out of the Mercury and shouted back toward Tepper. "It's your fault!" she said. "That should have been our spot! It's your fault. Making people waste time talking to you! You ought to be ashamed of yourself."

Tepper, pretending not to hear her, went back to his newspaper. He was reading a story about an office betting pool that had been held every week in a commodities-trading firm for as long as anyone in the firm could remember. A committee of the firm's partners met regularly to decide on each week's pool topic, always based on current events. The office pool had been a subject of press interest before. During the Vietnam War, some people objected to the pool's being based for several weeks in a row on casualty figures. One of the firm's partners responded by saying, "People who don't want to play hardball should get out of the game," but the casualty-figure pools were quietly dropped in favor of pools based on how many tons of explosives would be dropped on North Vietnam that week.

The commodity firm's pool was back in the news because it had been based that week on how many people would be cited for hailing a taxicab incorrectly. The mayor, Frank Ducavelli, as part of his never-ending campaign to make the city more orderly, had declared a crackdown on people who stepped out in the street to hail a taxi rather than remaining on the curb, as required by an ordinance that nobody but the mayor and his city attorney had ever heard of. Tabloid headlines didn't have the space for the mayor's entire last name. It was known that when Frank Ducavelli first became a force in the city he had hoped that headline writers might refer to him as the Duke, suggesting not only nobility but the Dodger great Duke Snider. Given the mayor's interest in order and his draconian response to anyone who disagreed with him, though, the tabloids tended to go with Il Duce. The item Tepper was reading about the weekly pool at the commodities-trading firm was headlined IL DUCE EDICT HOT COMMODITY.

The taxi drivers had objected to the enforcement of the ordinance, of course, and the mayor had called them vermin. The senior staff attorney of the New York Civil Liberties Union,

Jeremy Thornton, had said that Ducavelli's attempt to enforce the ordinance was "another of the spitballs that our mayor regularly flings at the Constitution of the United States." The mayor had replied that Jeremy Thornton had a constitutional right to demonstrate that he was a reckless and irresponsible fool but that he should probably be disbarred anyway, as a public service. When a city councilman, Norm Plotkin, usually a supporter of City Hall, pointed out that someone flagging a cab from behind a line of parked cars was unlikely to be seen, he had been dismissed by Mayor Ducavelli as "stupid and imbecilic—someone who obviously has no regard whatsoever for public safety and is totally unconcerned about citizens of this city being struck down and killed in the street like dogs."

Years before, in an article about how jokes get created and spread around, Tepper had read that commodities traders were at the heart of the joke distribution system. The article had inspired him to test a list of licensed commodities brokers for a client who was trying to sell a book of elephant jokes through the mail, and the list had done fairly well—well enough to justify its use again to sell a book of lightbulb jokes and a tape-cassette course on how to be a hit at parties. Tepper had decided that the actual trading of commodities must not require a lot of time if traders could engage in so many extracurricular activities, like organizing betting pools and distributing jokes.

Tepper could hear the drone of another car moving slowly down the street behind him. He decided to use the backhand flick if the car stopped next to him. He had perfected the backhand flick only that week—a speeded-up version of someone clearing away cobwebs while walking through a dimly lit attic. He used only his left hand. Without looking up from his newspaper, he would flick his fingers in the direction of the inquiring parker. It had taken some time to find precisely the right velocity of flicking—a movement that contained authority but lacked aggression.

The first time he had used the backhand flick—it was on Fifty-seventh Street, between Tenth and Eleventh avenues, around the dinner hour—he had obviously flicked too aggressively. The gesture had brought a fat, red-faced man out of a huge sport-utility vehicle—a vehicle so high off the ground that the fat man, before laboriously lowering himself to the pavement, hovered in the doorway like a parachutist who'd taken a moment to reconsider before deciding that he did indeed want to leap out into thin air. Once on terra firma, the fat man had stood a few inches from Tepper's window, which was closed, and shouted, "Ya jerky bastard, ya!" again and again. Tepper was interested to hear the expression "ya jerky bastard, ya"—he hadn't heard it used since the old days at Ebbets Field—but he did recognize the need to flick his hand more subtly. Tepper hadn't replied to the fat man, and not simply because there really didn't seem to be any appropriate reply to "ya jerky bastard, ya." Tepper tried to avoid speaking to the people who wanted to park in his spot.

2. *Linda*

BY GLANCING AT HIS SIDE MIRROR, TEPPER GOT A GOOD view of the car that had stopped one spot behind him and then slowly moved up to pull even with the Chevy. It was a sports car driven by one of those young men who dress in nothing but black; Tepper had seen pictures of them standing in groups in front of late-night clubs downtown, barely visible in their black clothing against the dark façades of the buildings. He often wondered what clothing-store clerks said when one of them came in to look around: "Something in black, sir?" Or "How about this lovely number in black?" Or "We've just gotten in some shirts in the most stunning shade of black." Whenever Tepper saw two or three people all in black walking together, he wondered if they lived together and, if so, what they did about folding and distributing the laundry that came out of their dryer. Wouldn't it all look alike? How many hours must they spend every week sorting it out? In his younger days, he'd associated black clothing with funerals, and sometimes, when he was driving through Tribeca or Chelsea, he'd see a large group of young people in black in front of an art gallery or a trendy restaurant and think for a moment that he was observing a throng of improbably young mourners.

The window of the sports car was rolled down and the driver began honking. Tepper continued reading the paper. "Hey, are you going out or not, man?" the driver of the sports car said loudly. "Or is that where you live? Is that car, like, rent-controlled?"

Even if Tepper talked to people who wanted to park in his space, he wouldn't have been certain how to tell the young man to leave. The phrases that he'd used in his own youth for such situations—"G'wan, giddoudahere!" came immediately to mind—would have probably sounded quaint rather than threatening to a young man in black, as if someone had shouted "Forsooth!" The problem was solved when the sports car peeled off suddenly, as if in a drag race.

After the sports car had left, Tepper heard the sound of another car approaching slowly from Fifth Avenue. He prepared himself for a firm but unthreatening backhand flick. The car pulled to a stop next to his Chevy; he could sense its bulk even though he kept his eyes on his paper. There were two quick honks. Most people honked twice—short, almost friendly honks. Some people leaned on the horn right away, angry even before Tepper wagged his finger or flicked his hand in the negative. Tepper waited for the second series of honks, then gave the honker a backhand flick.

There were two more short honks. Then a series of three. Then six. Tepper, scratching his head in a way that permitted him to obscure his eyes, took a quick peek at the car next to him. It was a red Volvo with a ski rack on it. Tepper took another quick glance at the front seat. Behind the wheel was his daughter, Linda. She was leaning across the seat toward him; she was rolling down the passenger-side window.

"Hi, Daddy," she said.

"I'm not going out," Tepper said.

"Daddy, it's me—Linda," his daughter said.

"I recognized you. One of the advantages of having only one daughter is that remembering her name and what she looks like is not difficult. Are you looking for a spot?"

"Of course I'm not looking for a spot, Daddy. Be serious."

"If you are, it's good here after six. But I'm not going out."

"Daddy, I wasn't looking for a spot. I was looking for you."

"What have you done with my grandson?" Tepper said. "Did he run away from home? Have you put him in foster care?"

"I think he's planning to wait until he's old enough to read the street signs before he runs away from home," Linda said. "Is that what you're doing, Daddy, running away from home?"

"Oh, no. I'm just parking, Linda. Later, I'm going back home."

"Let me get this straight," Linda said. "You go from the office to the garage that you pay for by the month, you get your car out, and you park it where you have no particular reason to be?"

"Well, now I've got a dollar and a half invested in this spot," Tepper said. "So there's good reason to be here at least until I get my money's worth. I read somewhere that the aggregate value of unexpired time left on meters people drive off from, just in New York alone, is the equivalent of the gross national product of something like thirty-eight different countries. I'll admit that it's hard to figure out what you're supposed to make of that statistic. I mean, it's not as if we could help the economy of those countries by staying longer at the meters. But there it is."

"Daddy, I'm not sure I understand what you're doing here," Linda said. "I mean, I remember when you used to keep the car on the street and switch it from one side of the street to the other every night, because of the alternate-side parking rules. I remember when I was a little girl sometimes Mom and I would have to wait dinner for you while you looked for a place to park that would be legal for the next day. And then you'd come in and you'd say, 'Guess what? A beautiful spot!' That was nice. You managed to keep the car on the street, and every night you had a little victory. Or maybe I just remember the victories. Maybe there were nights when you looked and looked and had to give up."

"That's one of the odd things about alternate-side parking," Tepper said. "There isn't exactly any way to give up."

Even so, he sometimes missed those evenings circling the blocks of the Upper West Side. Most of the neighborhood was governed by alternate-side parking regulations, for street-cleaning purposes, and he knew from long experience which sides of which streets said, NO PARKING 8AM–11AM MON–WED–FRI, and which said, TUES–THURS–SAT, and which said, improbably, MON–THURS or TUE–FRI, and which, just to keep you on your toes, said, 11AM–2PM instead of 8AM–11AM. What he often had trouble keeping in his mind was which day of the week the next day—the relevant day—would be, and he was in the habit of repeating it, half under his breath, as he searched for a spot regulated by a sign that did not mention it.

As he moved down the street, looking for a spot that alternate-side parkers call "good for tomorrow," he'd say "Tuesday, Tuesday, Tuesday" over and over, almost as if he were chanting some sort of mantra. He'd listen intently for the sound of an ignition being turned. He'd glance quickly from side to side, hoping to spot the flicker of a dashboard light that would indicate someone had just opened a car door and might be about to pull out. There were nights when he was totally confident of finding a spot. There were nights when he could almost imagine himself with a large tattoo on his arm that said, BORN TO PARK. There were nights when he knew that it was only a matter of time before he'd slip into a NO PARKING MON—WED—FRI spot, emitting, as the car came to rest against the curb, a final "Tuesday!" loud enough to startle passersby.

"But then you were finding a parking spot because you needed one," Linda was saying. "You don't need a spot on Forty-third Street. You don't even need a spot near home, Daddy. You keep the car in a garage now."

Tepper thought about that. "I suppose you could say that getting the garage meant that I finally figured out how to give up, for good."

"It's nothing to be ashamed of, Daddy. You just found better things to do with your time than circling block after block looking for a parking space."

Tepper was silent for a while. Then he said, "I suppose your mother sent you."

"Well, she did call," Linda said. "She asked me what she should do and I asked Richard and Richard said she should give you some space. But I thought I'd just come over and see if you were okay."

Tepper chuckled. "Well, you can tell Richard that I've got a space here," he said. "But I'm not going out."

"Daddy, you can't expect Mom to understand what's going on when you say, 'I think I'll go park on Forty-third Street for a while.'"

"I always like her to know where I am. Otherwise, she worries."

Behind the narrow lane left by their two cars, a Toyota slowed to a stop. The driver honked his horn. Linda didn't seem to hear. Tepper gave the Toyota a backhand flick. The driver shrugged, and moved carefully past Linda's Volvo with five or six inches to spare on either side.

"Daddy, I don't want to be pushy or anything," Linda said, "but what if I asked a fairly direct question: What, exactly, are you doing here?"

"I was reading the *Post*," Tepper said.

Neither of them said anything for a few moments. The only sound was the idling of the Volvo's engine. "Daddy," Linda said after a while. "You're not trying to relive those days, are you? I mean the days when you used to look for a beautiful spot every night, while Mom and I got dinner ready."

"You mean like some old duffer who keeps thinking of the glories of his high-school football triumphs and ends up drunk late at night on the football field of his youth?"

"Well, yes," she said. "Sort of. Except not drunk."

"Linda, let me explain something to you," he said. "It's something we probably should have gotten straight a long time ago. The parking I did then was alternate-side parking. This is meters. This is an entirely different situation."

"Do you know what Aunt Harriet told Mom?" Linda asked.

"I can imagine."

"She said that you're subconsciously punishing Mom for all those nights she goes off and plays bridge."

"Listen, her partner has always been Aunt Harriet," Tepper said. "I figure that was punishment enough."

Linda laughed. Then she grew serious again. "Daddy," she said, "you're not having some sort of midlife crisis, are you?"

"Well, I'm sixty-seven years old," Tepper said. "So the math alone makes it unlikely, I think. It's much more likely that I'm just sitting here reading the paper."

"Daddy, what should I tell Mom?"

"You could tell her that I'm on Forty-third Street, parking," Tepper said. "But, of course, I've already told her that. Maybe you could say that you've confirmed that I'm on Forty-third Street, parking. I don't like her to worry."

3. *Il Duce*

AS MIKE SHANAHAN APPROACHED CITY HALL, HE WAS struck again by the extraordinary precautions Frank Ducavelli had taken against an eruption of what the mayor always called "the forces of disorder." Although the closest City Hall had come to being stormed during the Ducavelli administration was a gathering of a few dozen noisy but peaceful citizens protesting the closing of a city day-care center in the district of a councilman who had defied the mayor, a forbidding steel fence had been erected at the perimeter of the lawn. Just inside the fence was an eight-foot field of concertina barbed wire. The graceful old building was beginning to look like the temporary headquarters of an invading army during some particularly nasty war. Shanahan, of course, knew it as the headquarters of a prosperous city that was, though eternally contentious, relatively peaceful— a city that had been spared the most serious turmoil of the brutish century that was drawing to a close.

He arrived at the narrow opening where visitors who had successfully made their way past a metal detector could pass through a turnstile onto the grounds, once the policeman who controlled the bar of the turnstile from an adjoining booth was convinced that all of the criteria for entry had been satisfied.

"Hiya, Eddie," Mike Shanahan said to the policeman, as he got out the picture ID that showed him to be a consultant to the mayor's office.

"How you doin', Mikey," the policeman said. The bar remained across the turnstile.

"You want to let me in, Eddie, so I can serve the people of this great city to the best of my ability?"

"We got a security check goin' today, Mike," the policeman said.

He began typing with two fingers on a computer keyboard in order to bring Shanahan's security form up on a monitor that only he could see.

"Didn't we have a security check yesterday?" Shanahan asked.

"That's right. So far, we've had a security check every day this week."

"The mayor particularly worried about the forces of disorder this week?"

"You got it," the policeman said. "Okay. Here we are. Grandmother's maiden name?"

"Eddie, listen: We grew up together. You actually *knew* my grandmother. Do I really have to tell you her maiden name every day?"

Eddie waited at the computer. Neither he nor Shanahan said anything for a few moments. Finally, Eddie said, "It's a job, Mikey."

"Houlihan," Shanahan said. "My grandmother's maiden name was Kate Houlihan."

"And an old dear she was, too," the policeman said, smiling at the memory. "I can still taste those molasses cookies of hers."

He asked Shanahan four more questions that were answered correctly, and then pressed a button to lower the bar on the turnstile. "Take her easy, Mikey," he said, as Shanahan walked toward the building.

Shanahan, showing his pass two or three more times to people he'd worked with for three years, finally made his way to the mayor's outer office, where Teresa, a secretary he'd slept with off and on for a period of four months earlier in the administration, informed him that any visitor to the mayor's office was now required to peer into a machine that would determine by the iris of his right eye whether or not he was who he said he was.

Shanahan looked at Teresa for a while without saying anything.

Teresa broke the silence. "If what I am witnessing constitutes being rendered speechless by news of this security device," she said, "you should know that being speechless is not a valid excuse. You still have to look into the machine."

"Do you have reason to believe I'm not me?" Shanahan asked.

"I'm pretty sure you're you," Teresa said. "How many people could look that much like the farmer driven out of Ireland by the potato famine? But if you don't let the machine check the iris of your right eye you can't go into the mayor's office."

Shanahan looked at the machine, which hadn't been there the day before. "How do you know what the iris of my right eye is supposed to look like?" he said.

"We got a baseline for everyone when you took your picture for the photo ID at the beginning of the administration," Teresa said, brightly. "Remember that second shot that seemed like a real close-up?"

"But that was three years ago," Mike said. "You mean the mayor was this worried about the forces of disorder three years ago?"

"Just look into the machine, willya, Mike? I've got a lot to do today. I've got you down here for ten o'clock. He'll be with you as soon as he's through with the parking commissioner."

Shanahan stared into the iris-identification machine, which gave a satisfying buzz signifying a matchup. Then he sank down into a chair next to Teresa's desk. She didn't look up as he muttered, "The mayor was thinking of this sort of thing three years ago." Three years before, in winning a campaign for City Hall against Bill Carmody, Frank Ducavelli had struck Mike Shanahan as relatively rational—tightly wound perhaps, maybe a bit moralistic at times, maybe a little too convinced of the uniqueness of his own level of rectitude, but basically a sensible man who had some good ideas for the city.

A moderate level of rationality had been what Shanahan was looking for in a mayoral candidate to work for. He had become tired of mayors like Bill Carmody who felt they had to be characters. Carmody had been frank about his efforts to be colorful. "People realize that a city like this is basically ungovernable, so they figure at least they might as well have a little entertainment," he'd once told Shanahan. "I don't know why I use the word 'govern.' What they really expect of a mayor is to get the garbage picked up and avoid subway strikes. This requires what the seminar people call public policy decisions? I don't think so, Michael. The public policy regarding garbage is to pick up the garbage." Among other eccentricities, Carmody wrote and sang songs with urban themes but country rhythms—cowboy laments on subjects like subway breakdowns or deli lines. He liked to describe himself as La Guardiaesque. In the *Daily News*, Ray Fannon, taking advantage of the fact that of one of the city's three airports had been named after the Little Flower, once wrote in his column, "Mayor Carmody is not La Guardiaesque and he's not Kennedyesque. Newarkesque he may be."

Shanahan, who had been in New York politics all of his life, mostly as a pollster, hadn't been certain that Bill Carmody was wrong in his analysis of the state of urban management. But it had seemed too early to give up on the possibility of governing a modern American city. In Frank Ducavelli, Shanahan had seen a man of enormous energy who obviously would never give up. He hadn't realized that in electing Ducavelli to replace Carmody the city could be going from a mayor who burst into song at City Hall ceremonies to a man who would try to pass an ordinance prohibiting singing on the public streets. Mayor Ducavelli, as it turned out, saw singing on the street as behavior that might seem trivial at first glance but could actually jar open the gates to the forces of disorder. Shanahan had once read a theory that every presidential administration makes you nostalgic for the administration that preceded it. He wondered if the theory could be extended to City Hall administrations.

"I now remember a part of that novel I'd forgotten," he said, out loud. "Those naval officers on the *Caine* had great contempt for the first captain they had, because he was lackadaisical, sloppy, all that. They were very relieved when he was replaced by a captain who did things by the book . . ."

"What are you muttering about there?" Teresa said.

". . . replaced by Captain Queeg."

A light flashed on Teresa's desk, and she said, "The mayor's ready for you now." At that moment, the parking commissioner, a nervous-looking man named Mark Simpkins, came out of the mayor's office and rushed past them, apparently too distraught to note their presence.

"He must have confessed that he took that helping of strawberries from the officers' mess," Shanahan said.

"What?" Teresa said.

"Here I go," Shanahan said, and entered the office. It was a large, paneled office, furnished with comfortable-looking leather chairs and, at one end, a conference table. There was a huge desk near one wall, but the mayor was not sitting behind it. He was pacing up and down, usually a sign that he was upset about something. In recent months, Shanahan had always found him pacing in front of his desk. Frank Ducavelli was, as it happened, a rather awkward pacer. In general his movements seemed jerky; Ray Fannon had once written that the mayor in movement "showed signs of having studied under the same ballet master as Richard M. Nixon." Ducavelli was in one of his trademark blue suits, which, like Nixon's suits, were often spoken of as looking as if the hanger got left in.

"Simpkins should have nailed those Ukrainians by now," Mayor Ducavelli said as Shanahan entered. "He treated them with kid gloves. You can't handle people like that with courtesy. They're animals. They have no respect for order. They're corrupt and despicable. Simpkins has to think of a way. We've got to nail those Ukrainians."

Ukraine was among the worst offenders when it came to parking tickets ignored by United Nations diplomats, all of whom claimed diplomatic immunity, and, for reasons nobody on the City Hall staff fully understood, the mayor had singled out the Ukrainian delegation as the prime target for his retaliation. To the mayor's frustration, though, a way to nail the Ukrainians had not been found. For a while, Ducavelli had put his hopes in a plan devised by the city attorney, Victor Hessbaugh. Under Hessbaugh's scheme, the city would haul away illegally parked cars of Ukrainian diplomats and claim that what had to be paid to get them back was a hauling and storage fee rather than a fine, and thus was not covered by the diplomatic immunity treaties. The Ukrainians had gone to court, bolstered by an amicus curiae brief from the counsel of the U.S. State Department, and a federal judge had granted them a restraining order against the mayor and his agents, ruling that the hauling and storage fee was simply a fine masquerading as something else. When the restraining order was handed down, the mayor had thrown what Teresa referred to as "one of his hissy fits." Shanahan had been in the office at the time. First, the mayor began carrying on about the judge, shouting, "The man's absolutely out of his mind" and "The judiciary has crumbled" and "The man has absolutely not a scintilla of understanding of the law." Then he started on the Ukrainians. "This is war!" he shouted. "This is war!"

After the mayor had calmed down enough to allow a word or two from others, Shanahan had offered some words of restraint: "Even if the behavior of the Ukrainians justifies an armed response, Mr. Mayor, I think I should remind you that Ukraine still has any number of nuclear weapons left over from the days of the old Soviet Union, and the city of New York, where people like to say that absolutely anything is available if you're willing to pay for it, has no nuclear weapons at all." That court decision had been a year and a half ago. Shanahan had let himself believe that

Mayor Ducavelli was no longer carrying a grudge against the Ukrainians—wishful thinking, he now realized, since he had learned long ago that the mayor's grudges were permanent.

"He's going to have to figure out some way to nail those Ukrainians," the mayor said again. "Parking is the key. That's where the disorder starts. Traffic's important, too. Never sell traffic short. Which is why we have to nail Norm Plotkin. Anybody who would attack a campaign to establish order in taxi-hailing around here is a deeply flawed human being. An irredeemably flawed human being. Worthless. Despicable. We ought to put a homeless shelter in his neighborhood. Actually, that's not a bad idea for the Ukrainians. A homeless shelter. That'll nail them. I'm going to put that in the works."

With that, the mayor returned to his desk and began scrawling a memo. He seemed to have forgotten Shanahan's presence. Shanahan, who had no idea why he'd been summoned in the first place, hadn't uttered a word. For a while, as Ducavelli scrawled furiously on a yellow legal pad, Shanahan watched him, occasionally trying to get his attention with a quiet "Mayor?" There was no response. Finally, Shanahan shrugged and left the office.

4.   *Salmon Slicer*

THAT SUNDAY, IN FRONT OF RUSS & DAUGHTERS APPE-
tizing store on Houston Street, one of the more desirable
Sunday-morning parking spots on the Lower East Side, Tepper
gave a silent shake of the head to a Dodge Dart, and then recognized it as the car he had given a wagging index finger to in
the same spot the previous Sunday. Was he getting repeaters?
Sooner or later they would presumably expect him to offer some
explanation of why he happened to be sitting in his car at the
same spot—perhaps that he was waiting for an elderly aunt from
Riverdale whose only outing of the week was a trip back to the
Lower East Side for a few bagels and a piece of kippered lox. But
he had no intention of offering any explanation at all. There was
no law that required explanations to owners of Dodge Darts. He
was in a legal parking spot. He had put a quarter in the meter. He
was paid up.

Apparently, the driver of the car right in front of him had not
been paid up. A meter maid was writing out a ticket, ignoring the
arguments of a skinny man who was practically shouting in her
ear. "I just went to get change," the skinny man said. "Look!
Here's the change! Here's four quarters in my hand. Change for
a dollar. Isn't that proof? What kind of person would just happen

to have four quarters in his pocket? Nobody, that's who. I was just going to get change."

The meter maid continued to write the ticket, paying no attention at all to the skinny man shouting at her from a few inches away. It was as if he didn't exist. When she got through, she double-checked the license plate against the ticket one more time. She didn't hand him the ticket. She put it under the windshield wiper on the driver's side. Then she walked down Houston Street to check the next meter. She still hadn't looked at the skinny man. He shouted after her. His tone had turned sarcastic. "You couldn't just ask the counterman if I'd just asked him for change," he said. "That would be much too much trouble. Couldn't just ask. You have no use for eyewitness testimony. No, not you."

Tepper went back to reading the Sunday *Post.* The headline on the story he was reading said, COMMISH FORFEITS SKIN GAME TO IL DUCE. Mayor Ducavelli had fired the parks commissioner, Cary Fox, because of the way Fox had responded to the mayor's order to draft a dress code that would ensure a higher standard of modesty in the city's parks. Apparently, the mayor had gone to Prospect Park, in Brooklyn, one warm Saturday for a ceremony and had been appalled at the skimpy costumes worn by some people who were jogging or flipping Frisbees or just lolling on the grass. The mayor had been dressed in a dark gray suit himself, although he'd made some concessions to the informality of the setting by leaving off his tie and unbuttoning the collar of his shirt. Describing the dress of some park users as "disgusting and depraved," Mayor Ducavelli had ordered Commissioner Fox to establish a detailed dress code that would be firmly enforced, with jail terms on the second offense.

Apparently because of suspicions that the parks department was dragging its feet on drafting the dress code, Fox had been called to City Hall by Mayor Ducavelli to present a progress report. During the presentation, while trying to explain a difficult paragraph that discussed a variety of measurements outlining how many inches from what would constitute thorough coverage of genitalia, Commissioner Fox had burst out laughing. The next morning it was announced in the pressroom that the mayor had accepted the resignation of Cary Fox. City Hall had denied that Fox's laughter was what brought about his dismissal, but the headline on the front page of the *Sunday News*, which Tepper had already finished and tossed over on the passenger seat, said, IL DUCE'S LAST LAUGH.

As Tepper glanced over at the *News*, it occurred to him that he had somehow missed reading Ray Fannon, who always appeared on Sunday. Fannon had emerged as the mayor's most persistent critic. Tepper picked up the *News* from the seat and turned to Fannon's column. "This latest firing could mean the eventual dissolution of the mayor's cabinet and the City Hall staff," Fannon had written, "since it is increasingly difficult for people who are in Frank Ducavelli's presence to keep a straight face."

Tepper, who always followed the goings-on in City Hall carefully, had been struck by the differing views of proper attire expressed by Mayor Ducavelli and his predecessor, Bill Carmody, who had taken such great delight in being considered a character. At a ceremony that took place in Prospect Park, Carmody would undoubtedly have worn what he referred to as his outdoor clothes—a baseball cap picked up from a catfish festival or a recreational vehicle park or an exterminating company, a T-shirt advertising Red Man chewing tobacco or a topless bar in

Daytona Beach, and, if the weather threatened to turn nippy, maybe a warm-up jacket that had block letters across the back saying PASSAIC AUTO BODY and script on the left breast spelling out *Rocco*. "At an outdoor ceremony, you can read the mayor," Tepper had once heard Ray Fannon say of Bill Carmody during a television roundtable. "I don't mean you can look into his eyes and divine his motives, because when you look into his eyes you see absolutely nothing. I mean that he's got enough writing on him so if you want to pass a few minutes before the speeches start, you can read him."

As Tepper glanced up from the newspaper to make a quick perusal of the Sunday shoppers, he noticed that one of the countermen from Russ & Daughters was standing on the sidewalk, about to tap on the window. Recognizing the counterman from past trips, Tepper slid over toward the passenger door and rolled the window down.

"How you doin'?" the counterman said, bending down to lean on the door.

"Fine," Tepper said. "How are you?"

"I thought I recognized you," the counterman said. "You come in to buy lox sometimes on Sunday."

"Herring salad usually," Tepper said. "Sometimes a whitefish. Very occasionally, lox."

"I've noticed you out here for a few Sundays now," the counterman said. "I figured maybe you're having trouble getting around or something, and I could get you something. We've got some whitefish today. Also sturgeon. The sturgeon here is terrific—sort of a specialty."

"Not even sort of a specialty—precisely a specialty," Tepper said. "I remember when the shopping bags used to say Russ &

Daughters: Queens of Lake Sturgeon. Now that was a shopping bag! No cute design. No curlicues. No website mentioned. No plastic. Just an honest brown paper bag, with handles that held some weight, and a straightforward motto—RUSS & DAUGHTERS: QUEENS OF LAKE STURGEON."

"Hey, you *are* an old customer. That was a while back. I could get you some sturgeon. Or herring salad."

"Thanks anyway," Tepper said. "I don't think anything today."

The counterman started to straighten up. Then he said, "Are you waiting for somebody?"

"No," Tepper said.

"Oh. Well . . . ," the counterman said. "Guess I should get back." But he made no move to leave. He smiled, in a friendly way. Finally, he said, "Just here, parking?"

"Exactly," Tepper said. "I'm just here, parking."

The counterman didn't say anything for a while. He was still leaning on the car door, looking in the window. Then he said, "You're just here parking because you feel like it, and if someone wants the spot, it's too bad, because it's your spot, and it's a legal spot—right?"

"Well," Tepper said. "The only thing you left out is that I put a quarter in the meter. So I'm paid up. Don't forget: the meters on the Lower East Side say, One Hour Parking, Nine A.M. to Seven P.M. *including* Sunday."

"You're absolutely right," the counterman said. "A lot of people don't know that, but you're absolutely right. Listen, a lot of times, I feel like doing something like this myself."

The counterman lapsed into silence again. Behind him, the skinny man who'd had the one-sided argument with the meter maid burst out of the door of Russ & Daughters. He wasn't carrying a shopping bag. Upset by his failure to convince the meter maid that he shouldn't be ticketed because he'd simply gone to get quarters, he had apparently gone back in the store without remembering to deposit one of those quarters in the meter; Tepper had actually been wondering if the meter maid, who was making her way back down the block, might put a second ticket on the skinny man's windshield. Before that could happen, though, the skinny man ran to the meter, quarters in hand; someone inside Russ & Daughters must have jogged his memory with one of those periodic announcements: "They're checking meters out there."

Finally, the counterman said, "You know, it can get pretty irritating with some of those customers."

"I'll bet," Tepper said.

"They'll say, 'Gimme a nice whitefish.' So I'll say, 'One whitefish, coming right up.' Cheerful. Pleasant. And they'll say, 'A *nice* whitefish.' Can you imagine? This happens every Sunday at least once. I could prevent it, of course. I could head it off. You know how I could prevent it . . ."

"Well," Tepper said. "I suppose—"

"Of course!" I could just repeat after them exactly: 'A nice whitefish.' But I won't. I won't give them the satisfaction. What I really feel like saying when they correct me—when I say, 'One whitefish, coming up,' and they say, 'A *nice* whitefish'—is, 'Oh? Well, I'm glad you said that, because I wasn't going to get you a *nice* whitefish. If you hadn't said that, I would have looked for a whitefish that's been sitting there since last Tish b'Ov—an old, greasy, *fershtunkene* whitefish. Because that's what we serve here mostly. That's our specialty. That's how we've managed to stay in business all these years. That's why the Russ family is synonymous with quality and integrity in this city for maybe seventy-five years—because they sell their steady customers rotten, stinking whitefish. That's why the boss gets up at four in the morning to go to the suppliers, so he can get the *fershtunkene* whitefish before his competitors. Otherwise, if he slept until a civilized hour, as maybe he deserves by now, he might get stuck with *nice* whitefish.'"

"There's always something," Tepper said.

The counterman, looking exhausted from his speech, could only nod and sigh. He glanced into the store and then looked back at Tepper. "Listen," he said. "Do you mind if I sit with you for a minute? It looks like it's quiet in there. I could take a little break."

"Why not?" Tepper said, opening the passenger door and sliding over to make room for the counterman.

"I shouldn't complain," the counterman said, when he had settled into the seat. "It's basically a nice place to work. Good people to work for. Most of the customers are fine. We get a lot of well-known people. Actors. Writers. People from the newspapers are always coming in. A lot of news people. Television news people. I actually enjoy my work, although I realized a long time ago that I have no natural talent for it."

"Talent?"

"Oh, I can slice lox well enough to satisfy the customers," the counterman said. "But have you ever seen Herman slice lox?"

"The one who used to wear the badge saying, HERMAN THE ARTISTIC SLICER?"

"Yes. A natural talent. They say you can read the *Times* through one of Herman's slices. You couldn't read anything through one of my slices. Oh, maybe one of those large-print editions, but I'm not kidding myself. No natural talent. Do you know what I really wanted to be? You'll never guess. An inventor."

Tepper would have never guessed. He studied the counterman—a stout man of about his own age, with gray hair and thick glasses. The counterman had a sort of stolid look. He looked like a counterman.

"Not Thomas Edison," the counterman said. "Not Alexander Graham Bell. I'm not kidding myself. But I thought I could invent little things that helped people out. That was my dream. But I didn't pursue it. It's probably hard for you to imagine; you're a man who does what he wants if he feels like doing it. I didn't pursue it. But that was my dream. Chemistry was my best subject. You know, I haven't mentioned this to anyone in years, but when I was a young man I came up with an invention I thought would go. I had this idea of inventing this soaking compound for soaking pots and pans. It had different chemicals that dissolved at different rates, so during the night this pot would be attacked steadily, and in the morning: zip, it's clean! I called it StediSoke, spelled S-t-e-d-i-S-o-k-e. I knew it would work, if I just put enough time in on the chemicals. But I didn't stick with it. I didn't pursue it. Then, years later, I saw it advertised in a catalog—not the same name, of course, but the same sort of thing. I could still kick myself."

"Don't kick yourself," Tepper said. "It didn't sell."

"It didn't sell?"

"A dog," Tepper said. "We handled it. We tried a list of people who had sent away for pots and pans offered in gourmet kitchen catalogs. We tried the subscription list of a cooking magazine. We even tested a list that was described on the rate card as 'Fourteen thousand people in New England who have consulted a dermatologist during the past ten years'—figuring those people might be interested in something that could keep their hands out of hot water. Nothing. Maybe the people on those lists have maids to clean their pots and pans. Maybe most people take a little pot scrubbing for granted as a part of life. Whatever, the returns were terrible. Believe me, it was a dog."

"I thought it would work," the counterman said.

"It probably did work. It cleaned the pots. But here's one of the lessons of life I've learned in my business: If it works but you can't sell it, it might as well not work. This is what they call a free-market economy."

The counterman had cheered up considerably. "It didn't sell?" he asked again.

Tepper shook his head. "A nothing. A big nothing."

The counterman was smiling. "It probably lost money," he said. "It probably lost money! That's really very satisfying to hear. It probably lost money. I know it's terrible to take comfort in the business reversals of other people."

"With these particular people, it's not so terrible," Tepper said. "They were a pain to deal with, and, if I'm not mistaken, they still owe us."

The counterman nodded, and reached over to shake Tepper's hand. "Listen," he said. "I can't tell you how much this talk has meant to me. It was inspiring. I hope I didn't interrupt you."

"Not at all," Tepper said. "In fact, I think I'll come in with you for a minute. You made me hungry with that talk of whitefish. And I've got a good spot here—plenty of time on the meter."

"Good," the counterman said, opening the car door. "I'll get you a nice whitefish."

5.   *Lists*

AT ELEVEN THE NEXT MORNING, TEPPER LOOKED UP FROM his desk. Arnie Sarnow was standing in the doorway. Arnie held a handful of rate cards, and a computer printout and a clipboard. His collar was open and his tie was pulled down. His hair looked as if he'd been running his hands through it, or maybe trying to tear out a clump here and there. Tepper had been expecting him. Arnie almost always came in by around eleven in the morning, usually looking as if the day had already been almost too much for him.

"Can I interrupt you for a minute, Murray?" he said.

"Why not," Tepper said. It was what he always said.

Arnie came in. Tepper's office had a chair next to the desk and, in front of the single window, a table with three chairs gathered around it. The table was, as usual, cluttered with the old-fashioned rate cards that Tepper went through in deciding which lists might be worth testing for whatever was being sold through the mail. Each card described a list that was available for rental—"40,000 buyers of American Revolution decorations and memorabilia" or "61,000 buyers of discount automotive accessories" or "40,000 buyers of deodorizing shoe pads." As many years as Tepper had been looking through such cards, they still often made him think of the old Ed Sullivan variety show in the early days of television, and the impressions comics used to do of Sullivan telling the audience what wonders were in store for them next week: "On this stage, next week, 40,000 Egyptian dentists, simultaneously pulling infected molars . . ."

Arnie, as usual, plopped down in the chair next to Tepper's desk. "Barney Mittgin is trying to drive me crazy," he said.

Tepper nodded his head. "How long you been here now, Arnie?" he asked.

"Almost two and a half years."

"Well," Tepper said, "Howard and I started this business forty years ago. Barney Mittgin was one of our first clients. Came in maybe the second or third week we were open. He was trying to sell an apple corer then, as I remember."

"An apple corer?"

"Yeah, but it also made Christmas tree ornaments," Tepper said. "Mittgin always specialized in things that had two uses. He used to sell a candlesnuffer that also cut out melon chunks. Now he's got an attaché case that turns into a foldout computer table. Maybe the apple corer didn't make Christmas tree ornaments, now that I think of it. Maybe it made decorative fudge. A lot of the things Mittgin sells make things that are described as decorative. Anyway, it was one of the first things we worked on. So Barney Mittgin has been trying to drive Howard and me crazy for forty years. And here we are, despite his best efforts. Maybe we're not at the top of the charts for mental health, but we're not crazy. And don't forget: all that time there have been other things to drive us crazy: mechanical breakdowns in the fulfillment houses, lost mail, other irritating clients. Barney Mittgin has not been working alone. So forty years from now—

thirty-seven and a half, really, because he's already been at you for two and a half years—it's unlikely that you're going to have to be institutionalized, at least not from the effects of prolonged contact with Barney Mittgin. That should be a source of comfort to you."

"I never thought of it that way," Arnie said. He actually looked a little bit relieved. Tepper had found that Arnie was easily upset but just as easily calmed—someone who grasped a phrase of encouragement and nodded in relief, like a nervous traveler who has been reassured that he's on the right train after all.

"Unless you think Howard and I actually are a little crazy," Tepper said, after some consideration. "Then I suppose it wouldn't be a source of comfort."

"I thought maybe Barney got to be more of a pain in the ass over the years," Arnie said.

"Nope, he started out as a pain in the ass, and he's still a pain in the ass," Tepper said. "What's the item he's selling?"

"It's a sort of little balloon you wear around your neck, for sleeping on airplanes," Arnie said.

"You put it around your neck and supposedly you sleep better because your head doesn't loll over and when you wake up you don't have a stiff neck? Is that the one?"

"That's it," Arnie said.

"I've seen it in a million catalogs," Tepper said. "Also, it's in every airport gift shop. Also, some airline—I think it was El Al—used to give them away free to everyone in Business Class."

"Well, this one—"

"Don't tell me," Tepper said. "It has another function."

Arnie nodded his head. "It's got the layouts of six major airports on it," he said. "O'Hare, LAX, JFK, La Guardia, Dallas—

Fort Worth, and Atlanta. It shows which airlines are in which terminals, where the gates are—at least it does when it's completely blown up. If it isn't blown up perfectly, you can get a crease that'll hide a few gates, or maybe even an entire airline."

Tepper shook his head. "The thing is around your neck and the airport maps are on the thing and you're supposed to read the thing?" He pretended he was wearing a balloon around his neck and he was trying to read a map on the side of the balloon. Over the years, despite all evidence to the contrary, he had persisted in thinking that he might discover how Barney Mittgin's mind worked if he understood how the product worked.

Arnie shrugged. "I guess you read it before or after it's on your neck," he said. "When it's on your neck, you're supposed to be asleep."

Tepper nodded. "I didn't think of that," he said. "Well, it sounds like one of Barney's items all right. And the creases aren't our problem. So what's the problem?"

Arnie started going through the pile of rate cards he was holding. "Well, I started him out by testing a list we call '65,000 High-Income Individuals Who Have Joined a Frequent Flyer Program.'"

"Sounds fine so far."

"Then we also have a membership list of a couple of those airline clubs that have the special lounges in airports. I tested them."

"Good, good."

"Then we've got that list of people who have baggage late or lost or something at O'Hare and have to give their name and address and have it sent to them."

"I would have never thought of that. I suppose a lot of them may still be too mad to respond to anything, but maybe not. I don't suppose Barney's maps are detailed enough to show where you go to look for your lost baggage?"

Arnie shook his head. "Creases," he said. "But that lost luggage list was okay. Just okay. Not great. So far, none of these lists are testing great."

"Arnie, you've done just right," Tepper said. "You've done exactly what I would have done under the circumstances. If they're not testing well, it's because nobody wants to break his neck reading a map while he's supposed to be asleep."

"That's not what Barney said. He said I don't have any imagination." Arnie looked truly dejected again.

"Arnie," Tepper said. "May I ask you how old you are?"

"I'm thirty-one years old," Arnie said.

"Well, let an older man tell you one of the lessons of life," Tepper said. "Barney Mittgin is a schmuck. None of this has to do with you, none of it has to do with me, none of it has to do with Worldwide Lists, Inc. It may not even have anything to do with the creases. What it has to do with is the fact that Barney is a schmuck. He can't admit that what he's trying to sell is not so great, so he finds someone else to blame. Schmuck-like behavior. When there's a schmuck involved, you can't analyze a situation as if there weren't a schmuck involved. For you, the important life lesson is this: when there's a schmuck involved, don't take it personally."

Tepper could see Arnie brighten. "He's trying to drive me crazy," Arnie repeated, as if offering another piece of evidence for Tepper's theory.

"You tried luggage—right?" Tepper said. "I don't mean lost luggage. I mean luggage buyers."

"Oh, sure," Arnie said. "A list of people who had sent away for one of those under-the-seat suitcases. Also earplugs. A list of people who had ordered earplugs from a catalog. The customer list of one of those car services that mainly take people to the airport. Barney says it's all obvious."

"It's the way we work," Tepper said. "We start with the obvious. We make a little universe around this imaginary customer of whatever Mittgin's selling—in this case, someone trying to sleep on an airplane. So people who belong to frequent flyer programs are obviously in this universe. If there aren't enough people in the center of the universe, we just reach a little farther—where the population is thinner. Barney likes it when we find a little clot of people we didn't expect—maybe subscribers to the most sophisticated trade magazine for mainframe computer repair people, because those people are always traveling and they're usually tired and because of their technical bent they might actually be able to figure out Barney's maps. It gives him a thrill."

"He says you would have thought of something special," Arnie said. "Maybe people who have bought sleeping pills through the mail, or compasses."

"Compasses?"

"Barney says you make connections like that—maps, compasses."

"This is an interesting notion," Tepper said. "I like the idea of some software drummer who comes into O'Hare on United with twenty minutes to catch his connecting flight to Eau Claire, and he gets out his compass to find the gate. If it's a compass he bought from Barney, of course, it also doubles as an olive pitter or something, so even if the salesman misses the plane he's got something to do."

"Barney says you've got a sixth sense."

"If I had any sense at all, I'd have told Barney Mittgin to get lost years ago," Tepper said. "And I would be in another business."

"He calls you Magic Touch Tepper."

"I call him a schmuck," Tepper said.

Howard Gordon was standing at the door. "Am I interrupting?" he said.

"Come in, Howard," Tepper said. "We were just talking about your old friend Barney Mittgin."

"A schmuck," Howard said.

"That's the conclusion we came to," Tepper said.

"He sometimes refers to Murray as Magic Touch Tepper," Howard said to Arnie. "Or just Touch when he's feeling particularly friendly. He's even worse when he's feeling particularly friendly. What's he selling now?"

"One of those doodads you put around your neck to help you sleep on the plane," Tepper said.

"What else does it do?"

"Well, it's a very good thing to sit on for an extremely tiny person who's just had a hemorrhoid operation," Tepper said. "But Barney isn't pushing that use."

"I better get back to it," Arnie said. He gathered up his rate cards and got up.

"Arnie," Tepper said, as Sarnow reached the door. "Why don't you give a mainframe-computer-repair trade magazine list a shot?"

Arnie nodded. "Thanks, Murray," he said, as he left. "I'll try that."

Howard took his chair. "How's it going, Murray?" he said.

"Fine," Tepper said. "How about you?"

"It could be worse," Howard said.

"I found a couple of nice clean bird-book lists that seem to work for Murphy's binoculars," Tepper said. "Frankly, I think most of the names are from the time we used the list of people who had bought Murphy's binoculars to sell bird books, but Murphy seems happy. You probably ought to try billing him before he gets sad again."

Howard nodded. He looked sad himself. On the other hand, he usually looked sad. He was a mostly bald man—thin, except for a comfortable little spare tire that had gradually accumulated around his hips over the years. He often had a pair of reading glasses perched on the end of his nose. He had a wide mouth that turned downward at the edges, giving it the shape of a child's drawing of a very low mountain. Tepper assumed that Howard smiled occasionally, but he couldn't remember what one of Howard's smiles looked like. Tepper had seen Howard laugh once. It was when someone told them that the best list for selling subscriptions to Kiplinger's newsletter, an expensive Washington newsletter published for businessmen, was a list of people who had sent away for a device used to clip nose hair. Murray Tepper had laughed at that one himself. "There's a great life secret in there somewhere," Tepper had said at the time. "If only we knew what it was." But that had been decades ago. Murray knew Howard to be a reasonably contented man, but strangers were likely to respond to meeting him by saying that they hoped he got some good news soon.

Howard was silent for a while. He was looking down at the floor. Then, without looking up, he said, "Murray, I talked to Ruth about this parking business."

Tepper just nodded. Howard looked sadder than ever.

"You know I don't want to butt in," Howard continued. "That's how we've been partners all these years. Even here we don't interfere. You don't tell me how to do the money part. I don't tell you how to do the . . . the . . ."

"Magic?" Murray said.

Howard almost smiled. "Yeah, the magic," he said.

Tepper knew that what he did every day at Worldwide Lists was to Howard Gordon, if not magic, at least puzzling. Howard ran the financial and administrative side of the business with competence, but he had no understanding of mailing lists. He simply couldn't see the connections—even the obvious ones, like the one between binoculars and lists of people who'd bought bird books through the mail.

"So you and Ruth had a talk?"

"Yes, we had a little talk," Howard said. "I told her that I don't like to butt in. You do what you want, Murray. If you want to park, park. People do funny things at our age. If you wanted to start riding a motorcycle, I wouldn't say a word. Maybe I'd say, 'Wear a helmet, Murray.' Otherwise, nothing. If you got yourself a popsie on the side, I'd probably say a little something—out of respect to Ruth. I'd make my opinion clear one time, and then you'd do what you wanted. With this, I'm not even going to say anything once. If you want to park, park."

"Thank you, Howard," Tepper said, rather formally. "If you want to get a popsie, wear a helmet."

Howard looked up at Tepper, obviously puzzled.

"A little joke," Tepper explained.

Howard nodded. "The thing is, Murray," he went on, "I just want to know if there's any problem in the business that has to do with this parking. I mean, is there anything that's troubling you here? If there's anything I can do, any change . . ."

"No, there's nothing," Tepper said. "You're doing fine, Howard."

"I know this business hasn't been everything you hoped it would be when we started," Howard said. "I know you had big plans then: Worldwide Lists. The name you chose says it."

"Howard, we got that name because it was already on the door, from the ribbon company—Worldwide Ribbons and Bands. The 'Ribbons and Bands' part was in much smaller letters, and we just had them rubbed off. Remember? I wanted to call it T & G Lists. In fact, this name turned out to be much better. T & G Lists sounds like something dirty: 'They were involved in T & G and other lewd pursuits.'"

The former ribbons office had offered mainly the advantage of cheapness. It was in the West Twenties, then a nondescript area of small office buildings. Now the neighborhood was prospering, having somehow become attractive to publishers and graphics companies and advertising firms. It had occurred to Tepper more than once that had Worldwide Lists scraped up the money to put a down payment on the building all those years ago, it would have made more money in real estate than it had made in forty years or so of dealing in mailing lists. The cafés and coffee shops where Tepper and his partner would sometimes get a tuna-fish sandwich or a plate of lasagna for lunch were gradually being replaced by restaurants much talked about for offering, say, Korean fusion or neo–Latin American. Howard sometimes said that he had to walk six blocks now to find a restaurant where he could understand the menu.

Howard was silent for a while. Then he said, "My God, how much could we have saved by not having to redo one word on the door?"

"There were ashtrays, too," Tepper reminded him.

Howard nodded his head, somehow made to look sadder by the thought of ashtrays with WORLDWIDE on them.

"Believe me, Howard," Tepper said. "It has nothing to do with the business."

"I had sort of hoped that by now we'd be set if we wanted to quit working," Howard went on. "We're not quite there. We're not doing badly, considering everything, but we're not quite there. It might have been different if those huge computers the big guys have hadn't gotten so sophisticated. Now they've got these Internet sites hooked up so they can tell what someone orders and try to sell them something like it the next time they come on. It's not the same business it was, Murray. Fewer people interested in dealing with a small outfit that works a lot on instinct. The young people are now looking to the Internet altogether; they figure there's no future for direct mail."

"It's a living," Tepper said.

"It could be worse," Howard said.

He sat there for a while, saying nothing. Then he said, "So what was the other function of the thing Barney's selling?"

"It's got floor plans of six major airports on it," Tepper said.

Howard shook his head as he got up from the chair. "What a schmuck," he said.

6. *Jack*

AT EIGHT-THIRTY THAT EVENING, TEPPER WAS PARKED on East Seventy-eighth Street. Although he hadn't required a spot that was legal for the following day, a sign next to his car said NO PARKING 11AM–2PM MON & THURS. The spot, in other words, could be legally occupied for more than sixty hours. It was the sort of spot that would have excited him in the days when he was keeping the car on the street instead of in a garage. Although Ruth had almost from the start described his nightly search for a good-for-tomorrow spot as "more aggravation that you don't need," there were moments of it that he'd loved. On evenings when he wasn't in any hurry, he had actually found it relaxing, in an odd way. Inside the cocoon of his car, he would sort of tune out—shut himself off from other thoughts as he began to circle the blocks around his apartment, repeating the day he needed not to see mentioned on the sign. He was always reminded of the state of mind he'd been in during those searches when he heard a marathoner who was being interviewed on television talk about having an out-of-body experience.

He still grew nostalgic every year when, on one of the first days of January, *The New York Times* published a list of national and religious holidays for which alternate-side parking regulations would be suspended. He was never quite clear on exactly why the rules were suspended for, say, All Saints' Day or Shemini Atzeret, but he preferred to take it as a gesture of respect. The city was saying, "We know that a certain number of our citizens will be celebrating Id al-Adha today, and we want them to do so without the burden of worrying about which side of the street their cars are parked on." When Tepper kept his car on the street, he always clipped out the list and put it in his glove compartment, part of the information base he carried with him while looking for a spot. He had taken a certain amount of pride in knowing where the fire hydrants were and what the signs on each block said. His sweetest memories were the times when, having confidently passed up some outsider who had slowed up approaching a space that Tepper knew to be next to a fire hydrant, he'd found a spot just down the street—a spot the stranger would have captured if he had been familiar with the territory.

In those days, if Tepper had found a spot that was good for sixty hours, he would have taken particular care backing in close to the curb. If the spot were long enough, he might even go back and forth a bit after he got in, like a quarter-miler taking a victory lap around the track. Then he would have locked the car, giving the doors an extra try just to make sure, and gone back to the apartment, eager to tell Ruth and Linda the good news. "Beautiful spot!" he'd say, as soon as he got in the door. "Guess when I next have to move the car?"

"Not for a year," Linda would say, with a mischievous smile. "It's good for a year. So you have a perfect spot, except, of course, you can't use the car, because if you do you might lose the spot.

48

Oh, no! I just thought of something. You're going to have to move it for the state safety inspection in just a few months. I guess this is not such a great spot after all."

Now he was in a similarly remarkable spot in the East Seventies, and he smiled as he thought of the days when Linda was still at home to tease him about his parking triumphs. He read the *Post* for a while, and then spent a while watching a man across the street who had pulled into a spot and then appeared concerned about whether his car was parked too close to a fire hydrant. First, the man stood as far from the car as he could get, his back pressed against the wall of an apartment building, and tried to judge the distance between his front bumper and the hydrant. Then he came forward and paced off the distance. Then, apparently satisfied, he started to walk away. Then, after a few steps, he returned and, instead of pacing, measured by putting one foot directly in front of the other, in an awkward little mincing step between his car and the hydrant. Then, he got what seemed to be some ribbon out of his car, and started measuring with that, turning it over and over, since it was only about two feet long. Finally, he was able to walk away.

A few minutes later, Tepper heard a car slow down. It seemed to be stopping next to his Chevy. He pretended to be looking for something in the glove compartment. Then the honking started—honking unlike Tepper had heard before. There was a series of short, staccato honks followed by a long wail. Tepper was too surprised to disguise his interest. He sat up and looked over at the car.

"Twenty-two shorts and a long," the driver said. "The secret fraternity honk."

"Hello, Jack," Tepper said. "I thought you might be around sooner or later. What secret fraternity honk, by the way? We were never in any fraternity."

"Sh-h-h," Jack said, putting his finger in front of his mouth and looking around in mock concern that someone might overhear them. "That's the secret. I don't suppose you're going out soon, are you, Murray? That's a hell of a parking spot you've got there. Won't have to move until eleven o'clock Thursday morning. That's the sort of rare East Side spot that used to tempt you, I know, even if it was late at night and you were actually on your way back to the West Side to go home."

"No—sorry." Tepper said. "I'm not going out just yet."

"Hold it just a minute," Jack said. "I'm going to park this thing across the street, and then I'll join you for a minute."

"That's a hydrant across the street," Tepper said. "You better leave your flashers on."

"And draw attention to myself? Not a chance. I always park in front of hydrants. The secret is to park smack in front of them rather than just too near them. You have to go all the way. If you're just too near them, you get a ticket. If you're smack in front of them, the cop rolling down the street can't see that there's a hydrant there at all. You have to be brazen. That's my motto, in parking and in life: be brazen. I know you don't feel that way, Murray. I'm aware that, when it comes to parking, you like to play rough but clean, like the West Point football team. Not me. I'm brazen. Hold on. I'll be there in a second."

Jack parked his car across the street, pulling in just ahead of the car whose owner had been so concerned about being too close to the hydrant. Then he crossed the street and slid into the passenger's seat of the Chevy. For a long time he didn't say anything. At least it was a long time for Jack. Tepper had known Jack since childhood—they'd become close in Miss Goldhurst's class, in fifth grade—and was not accustomed to silence when Jack was around.

"I guess it's a nice quiet place to read the paper," Jack finally said. "Except for people asking you all the time if you're going out."

"It's okay," Tepper said. "And, as you say, it's good until Thursday."

"Anything special bothering you, Murray?" Jack said. "You and Ruth okay? She sounded a little worried when she called."

"Ruth?" Tepper said. "Ruth's fine. Still doing her painting. Yes, Ruth and I are okay."

"She says your son-in-law told her that what you might be doing is 'trying to exert some meaningful control over your environment,'" Jack said.

"Richard repeats a lot of phrases he reads in magazines," Tepper said. "He probably got that one out of an article on why it's good to make your kids clean up their rooms. My grandson's three years old, and it wouldn't surprise me if his father tells him to clean up his room because it's important to exert some meaningful control over your environment."

"Maybe he meant it in a nice way," Jack said. "Maybe when one of his tennis buddies says in the locker room, 'My father-in-law just did a fifty-million-dollar deal,' he says, 'Hey, that's nothing: Linda's dad is trying to exert some meaningful control over his environment.'"

"All those years I worried that Linda might marry a drunk or a thug or something," Tepper said. "I kept my eye out for some hood driving up on a Harley-Davidson. To this day, when I hear that roar that a big motorcycle makes, I think some big hairy slob wearing greasy blue jeans—what I believe they now call a biker dude—is coming to try to marry Linda. So what happens? No biker dude comes anywhere near Linda. A guy drives up in a Volvo and she marries him and he talks about 'meaningful control over your environment.' I feel like I was blindsided."

"That's not why you're here, though," Jack said, making it into more or less a question.

"No. Not really."

"Everything okay at the office? Are those turkeys still hiring you to sell their tchotchkes? They haven't caught on yet?"

"Yeah, it's all okay at the office," Tepper said. "Well, it's the same."

"I keep telling you that it's amazing you're still in business. First came computers. Now the Internet. That means that you and Howard are now at least two communications revolutions behind the times. You guys are operating a biplane there, Murray, in the middle of a lot of jumbo jets."

"We're flying below the radar," Tepper said. "There's always a little business below the radar."

"Is it the Dodgers, Murray? That's the only thing I could think of. Are you out here because you're still mad that they moved the Dodgers to L.A.? If you are, you know, it doesn't make any sense. You want to know why it doesn't make any sense? Because then you should be parking in Brooklyn, not on Seventy-eighth Street. So are you lost or what?"

Tepper smiled. "Jack," he said. "You were the one who got so mad when they moved the Dodgers to L.A."

Jack thought about that for a moment, and then nodded. "You're right," he said. "The bastards! But you don't find me still mad about it, right? I don't even care about them anymore. They lose a close one in the ninth, I couldn't care less. I care so little I even forgot that I was the one who was mad."

Jack didn't say anything for a while. A Honda honked behind them, and Tepper waved it on without looking back. "Nice place for a chat, guys," the driver of the Honda shouted, as he slowed to a stop in front of them. "Whatever happened to having a chat on a park bench? Whatever happened to having a chat on the stoop?" Then he moved on.

"Murray," Jack said, "there are a lot of little things that irritate all of us. Look, today, I paid my credit-card bills, and every single one of the envelopes had an ad attached that you had to tear off before you could seal the envelope. Here I am trying to send in a check for what I already bought, and before I can do it I have to tear off an ad for an attaché case that turns into a bridge table or some goddamn thing."

"A foldout computer table," Tepper said.

"What?"

"A foldout computer table. The attaché case turns into a foldout computer table. We handled that one."

"Right, a foldout computer table," Jack said. "Whatever."

Tepper nodded sympathetically. "There's always something," he said.

"But, Murray," Jack went on, "if you're irritated about something, there are really more direct ways to make your feelings known."

"You mean I should write letters, the way you wrote the owners of the Dodgers when they were talking about going to Los Angeles?"

"Because this doesn't really have any connection to the

people who are responsible for anything," Jack said. "That guy who just got so pissed off because you weren't going out almost certainly isn't the guy who puts ads on the envelopes for credit-card bills. He didn't move the Dodgers to Los Angeles."

"Probably not the Dodgers," Tepper said. "He seemed too young. Also, the people who moved the Dodgers to Los Angeles don't need a spot. There's valet parking in Los Angeles. You drive up to the door of the restaurant and some kid from Honduras drives your car away for you. You don't even know where it is. You know, it's conceivable that there are people in Los Angeles who have never actually seen their car when it's parked, except when it's inside their garage. That's very strange."

"That bastard from the Dodgers never even answered me," Jack said. "So does that mean I should go sit in my car in Times Square?"

"Times Square is all No Parking Anytime," Tepper said.

Jack considered that. "On the other hand, you're not harming anybody," he said. "I mean, they all find a spot eventually, or they give up."

"If they can figure out how," Tepper said.

"It's not like you're walking around with a sandwich sign like some nutso," Jack said. "Or calling in bomb threats."

Tepper didn't say anything. They sat in silence for a while. Finally, Jack shrugged, and said, "I don't see the harm."

"Is that going to be your report to Ruth?" Tepper asked. "You don't see the harm?"

"Well, I might dress it up a little," Jack said. "But, yeah, basically, that's going to be my report: I don't see the harm."

"Good," Tepper said.

"So you want to have a beer?" Jack asked. "It's early yet, and I found this bar on Third Avenue that doesn't treat mature gentlemen such as ourselves like old coots whose false teeth are about to fall into their beer. It's what they call a yuppie-free environment."

"Thanks anyway," Tepper said. "I'm not going out."

7.   *Poker Night*

"OKAY, MOISHE IN THE MIDDLE," CHUCK GOLD SAID, starting to deal the cards.

"Moishe in the Middle?" Mike Shanahan said. "I don't believe I'm familiar with Moishe in the Middle."

"What are you, Shanahan—some kind of rube?" said Gold, a City Hall reporter for the *Times*. "Everybody knows Moishe in the Middle. It's five-card draw except there's a card in the middle that can be used as a wild card. First you bet, then you draw, then you bet—just like regular five-card draw. Then you bet with the card down, then with the card showing."

"That's all?" Shanahan said.

"Then with the card down again."

"But we'll already know what it is," Shanahan said. "Why would you bet with the card down again?"

"Because the rules of Moishe in the Middle call for that," Gold replied, continuing to deal. At the Monday night poker game held at Ray Fannon's brownstone on East Seventy-eighth, the final hand was always some wild variety of poker that the dealer had learned in high school—an effort to attach a rather zany end to an evening that had consisted of hand after hand of purist five-card draw and five-card stud and seven-card stud.

Moishe in the Middle was, in fact, a relatively calm game for the final hand, which often featured games with names like Shipwreck and Indian and So's Your Mother.

When the hand of Moishe in the Middle was over, nobody moved. At Fannon's, players tended to linger at the table after the last hand had been played. Toting up the chips was accomplished at a stately pace. For anybody who wanted to tell an anecdote, this was the first opportunity of the evening to get all the way to the punch line without worrying about people saying, "Hey, I thought we came here to play poker!"—although there was still likely to be an interruption for some other reason. Chuck Gold, apparently feeling that he still held the floor from having presided over a hand of Moishe in the Middle, began reminiscing about a former mayor who liked to tell anybody he met how much he respected them—to the point that Fannon, in his *Daily News* column, had defined the mayor's goal as "making each and every resident of this city feel like the don of the Corleone family." The mention of a former mayor led naturally to a discussion of Frank Ducavelli. Those gathered around the table made predictions about how the taxi-hailing restrictions were likely to go. They discussed what could possibly make the mayor think that he could get away with blocking the promotion of one of his critics at City University on the grounds of "reckless insolence." They compared theories on what had happened to the mayor's campaign to enforce regulations requiring sidewalk hot dog vendors to wear gloves and to extend the regulations to a number of other occupations—a campaign that hadn't been heard of for a while, even though as recently as the previous January it had dominated the mayor's State of the City address.

"Jesus, I had almost forgotten that speech," Steve Lopez, a City Hall reporter from one of the local news channels, said. "The Naked Hands Speech!" In a column on the State of the City address, Ray Fannon had imagined the mayor unable to sleep at night, tossing and turning as he thought of all the naked hands in the city—hands that were kneading dough or selling subway tokens or receiving bank deposits or shaking other naked hands.

"Reluctant as I am to credit any of my clients with any sense at all," Shanahan said, "I do think it's possible that hizzoner may have realized that requiring gloves is not some sort of magic bullet in the battle for public health. The problem is that these guys wear gloves but they wear the same gloves all day. They handle the hot dogs with the gloves. They make change with the gloves. They scratch their ass with the gloves. As long as they've got gloves on, they think everything is dandy."

"You don't think dropping the glove business means that he might be thinking of running for governor or senator instead of mayor, do you?" Bart Adams, a political consultant, asked, as he made uniform stacks of the chips in front of him. "I mean, if you were going to run for senator you wouldn't want to be identified with some pissant issue like whether hot dog guys wear gloves."

"You mean as opposed to a substantial issue like whether people should hail taxis from the sidewalk instead of the street?" Fannon said. "Or a monumental, senatorial-level issue like whether there should be a zero-tolerance policy backed up by prison terms for display of butt-crack in a public park."

"I can't imagine him not running for mayor again," Shanahan said. "He loves being mayor."

"But will the Wacko run against him?" Gold asked. Bill Carmody, the man Ducavelli had defeated to become mayor, was also known as the Woodside Wacko or the Queens Cowboy or, in the Hasidic neighborhoods of Brooklyn, Der Mishuganer.

"I hear the Wacko has been working on more songs," Steve Lopez said. "That's a sure sign. Somebody told me he has a whole series of songs about subway stations—I suppose lines like 'My life began to be a mess / when I just missed the downtown express' and that sort of thing."

Apparently, Carmody had become a singing mayor after reading about Jimmie Davis, who had sung right through a term or two as governor of Louisiana. Ray Fannon had felt compelled to point out in print that before turning to politics Davis had made his living as a country singer and songwriter—someone who'd composed such classics as "You Are My Sunshine"—while the mayor had made his living as a Queens lawyer who specialized in real estate matters, particularly those that could best be taken care of by knowing some people at the Department of Buildings. Carmody had never seemed at all impressed by Fannon's reasoning. "It's true that I'm just an amateur songwriter," he'd said, in response to such criticism, "but I'm a pro when it comes to being mayor."

"I have to say that it's hard to forget that traffic jam lament he did at the Press Banquet—'We'll Never Be Bumper to Bumper Again,'" Fannon said.

Steve Lopez and Chuck Gold broke out in a loud, toneless rendition of everybody's favorite couplet from "We'll Never Be Bumper to Bumper Again": "I knew I had lost my sweet little Midge / When she said, 'I *told* you we shoulda took the bridge.'"

Carmody's urge to perform could come upon him at wildly disparate moments—while welcoming a visiting dignitary from a country whose officials normally didn't sing in public, for instance, or presiding over a long session with Jewish community leaders on the question of whether the Bronx needed its own Holocaust museum. Although he might hit a chord now and then on a guitar, the accompaniment was usually provided on the piano by an old Tin Pan Alley song plugger named Maxie Allen, who put Carmody's words to music. Maxie's work clothes consisted of a shiny black suit, a white shirt whose collar seemed too big, a tie decorated with musical notes, and false teeth of shocking whiteness. While Maxie Allen somehow wrung a country beat out of his tinny upright, the mayor sang of star-crossed lovers living out their days in separate rent-controlled apartments that they couldn't afford to leave ("until that sweet old man—so sad, so shy—/ Was finally called by the great decontroller in the sky"). He sang songs of triumphs on Wall Street and unrequited love at Upper East Side singles bars. Someone had described his style as "borough country."

"Remember that great exchange with the cardinal at the Catholic Charities dinner?" Lopez said.

The presence of the cardinal had always seemed to inspire the mayor to song. The cardinal was a tall, highly cultivated, distinguished-looking man. He was the son of an Irish fireman, and he was a champion of the city's working poor. But when he appeared in front of his flock, in the cathedral on Sundays or at the dinner of a Holy Name Society or the annual dance of an Irish county society practically any evening, he carried himself so regally that it was common for someone to comment that he looked like the Episcopal bishop who had wandered in by mistake.

"What was the exchange with the cardinal?" someone said, to Lopez's obvious delight.

"Just before the program, Carmody said, 'Maybe you'd like to hear a little tune I thought of after I was in a bad traffic jam just on the other side of the Midtown Tunnel, Your Eminence.'" Lopez said, "And the cardinal said, in that plummy, high-class accent of his, 'For a man in my position, Mr. Mayor, just about anything but "Danny Boy" would be a most welcome change of pace.'"

"I've got to say I sort of miss Der Mishuganer," Chuck Gold said.

"I don't miss that phony bastard at all," Brian Higgins, a *News* assistant city editor, said.

"You just didn't like the fact that he showed how powerless and irrelevant we jackals of the press really are," Gold said. "Every other week you'd send a reporter to Queens to find people who were baffled at how a man who had seemed like such a conventional schlub as a lawyer and a city councilman had somehow become the Woodside Wacko. And you'd run the story thinking, 'Everybody's going to see now how contrived all this is,' and, instead of denying anything about his past, the Wacko'd say something like, 'It's absolutely true that I was once a normal human being. This job would turn anyone into a nutcase.' And that would be that."

"Well, you're right that nobody seemed to care that Carmody wasn't really wacko," Higgins said. "Any more than anybody seems to care that Ducavelli really *is* wacko. So much for the power of the press."

"Il Duce is getting more paranoid by the minute," Fannon said.

"It's true that the last time I went in to see him I had to first confirm my identity on an iris matchup machine," Shanahan said. "But I'm proud to say that I passed quite nicely. I'm who I am."

"We've got something in the paper tomorrow about City Hall ordering one of those chairs you sit in and a buzzer goes off if there's anything hidden in a body orifice," Higgins said.

"You've got to be kidding," Fannon said.

"You mean it can spot a guy with a bug up his ass?" Gold said, and began to cackle at his own joke.

Everyone else groaned and got up from the table. As Fannon showed them out, they stood on his stoop for a few moments, happy to be in the spring evening's air after a couple of hours in the closed and smoky atmosphere of Fannon's parlor. Silently, they watched a sort of standoff across the street involving two parkers who had been going for the same spot. Apparently, one of the parkers had pulled up one car ahead of the spot to back in and the other had approached from the rear. Both cars were about a third of the way in, and both drivers were out of their cars. "I'm prepared to stay here all night, if necessary," one of them was saying.

"It figures," the other one replied. "What else would someone like you have to do?"

Three or four cars behind the standoff, a man was reading the *Post* while sitting behind the wheel of a parked Chevrolet. "Very clever of you to hire somebody to read the *Post* outside my house," Fannon said to the crowd at large. "Otherwise, I might get the impression that nobody at all reads that rag."

8. *Jeffrey Green*

THE DRIVER OF THE TOYOTA SEEMED ANGRY BEFORE HE even asked the question. He had pulled his car even with the Chevy Malibu that was parked in front of Russ & Daughters. He was scowling, and his voice, as it boomed out of the Toyota's front window, had an angry edge to it. "Are you going out or not?" he said.

Tepper smiled and shook his head—a small shake of the head, like a bidder at an auction responding in the negative when the auctioneer meets his eyes as a way of asking whether he wants to top a bid that has just topped his. Tepper had been practicing almost imperceptible headshakes.

"You're not going out?" the man in the Toyota said, as if he couldn't believe what he was hearing.

Tepper shook his head again, still smiling.

"Whadaya—live there?" the man shouted. "You one of these homeless bastards, except you've got a car?"

Tepper didn't answer, and the Toyota pulled away. Tepper went back to his paper. He was reading a story about a dispute between Frank Ducavelli and the editors of a publication called *Beautiful Spot: A Magazine of Parking.* In its latest issue, *Beautiful Spot* had published a long article entitled "How to Beat It"—an article that included step-by-step instructions on how to avoid paying each type of parking ticket issued by the city. The mayor, calling the article "a recipe for lawlessness," had banned the sale of *Beautiful Spot* at all newsstands in city buildings. Unsurprisingly, the magazine's editors had gone to court, citing First Amendment rights to free speech. The mayor had replied, "There is no right to sedition. There is no right to lawless anarchy." He'd reiterated his oft-stated belief that respect for the parking laws was the bedrock upon which modern urban civilization had to be built. Meanwhile, *Beautiful Spot* was unavailable in the newsstands of city buildings and, of course, sold out everywhere else. The headline on the story was IL DUCE INSISTS NO SPOT FOR PARKING MAG.

Tepper heard a knock on the passenger-side window and looked over. The counterman he'd met the week before was standing on the sidewalk. A young man stood next to him. Tepper rolled down the window.

"It's me," the counterman said. "I guess you're not going out—huh?" He smiled and winked in a knowing way.

"No, I'm not going out," Tepper said.

"Listen, that was a great talk we had last week," the counterman said. "I want to thank you for your help."

"I really didn't do anything . . ."

"No, no, what you said about that soaking compound not selling—that was like a gift to me," the counterman said.

"If stories about what didn't sell are considered gifts, someone in my line of work could be a great philanthropist," Tepper said.

"Listen, there's someone I'd like you to meet," the counterman said, nodding at the young man next to him. "This is my nephew, Jeffrey Green. My grandnephew, really. From Cleveland. But he lives here now. He wanted to meet you. Would it be okay if he sat with you for a few minutes?"

"Why not?" Tepper said, opening the door.

The counterman went back into the store, and Jeffrey Green got into the car. He was a cheerful looking young man in his early twenties, dressed informally but neatly. He had sandy hair and blue eyes and a sort of open expression that made him look as if he were always about to say, "Really! No kidding! How interesting!" He smiled at Tepper and shook hands. "I told my Uncle Irv I'd really be interested in meeting you," he said.

"I don't suppose you've got something you want to sell through the mails," Tepper said.

"Oh, no," Jeffrey said.

"A scheme for marketing StediSoke to Generation X?"

"No, nothing like that," Jeffrey said. "I'm sort of a reporter."

"Sort of?" Tepper said. "You mean you report part of the story and let the readers imagine the rest, or do you mean you don't have a job?"

"I guess it's closer to not having a job. At least a regular job. I'm a freelancer. I write feature stories mainly, around New York. But what I want to be is a political reporter. I'd like to cover congressional campaigns, maybe even presidential campaigns— that sort of thing. I did my thesis in journalism school on campaign coverage. I've got some ideas about political reporting that I'd really like to try out someday."

"I have one question I've been waiting to ask someone with your specialty," Tepper said. "Why is it that reporters covering an election campaign write almost exclusively about who might win, even though we're all going to know that the night of the election anyway?"

Jeffrey thought about the question for a while. Then he said, "I can't imagine."

"You sound like a sensible young man," Tepper said. "I was afraid you might think you know. What can I do for you?"

"I'd like to interview you for a story."

"My politics are simple. I'm a regular voter, and I usually regret my vote."

"No, the story wouldn't be about politics."

"Not about politics?"

"No. What I thought would be interesting to write about was what you're doing here."

"I was reading the paper," Tepper said.

"No, I mean why you're here, in this parking spot," Jeffrey said.

"Oh, it's a legal spot," Tepper said. "I've got thirty minutes left on the meter."

"Well, then, that would be in the article," Jeffrey said. "I think it's an interesting story, and I think I might be able to place it in this neighborhood paper I sometimes write for—the East Village *Rag.*"

"The paper calls itself a rag?" Tepper asked.

"Well, yes," Jeffrey said. "The editor thought of that. He says it's very postmodern."

"Postmodern?"

"I've never been quite sure what that means either," Jeffrey said. "The editor keeps saying that part of being postmodern is being self-referential. Also ironic. So the paper refers to itself, ironically, as the East Village *Rag*."

Tepper nodded. "You might say the East Village is post-modern itself," he said. "Just a few years ago, in what we all thought were modern times, there wasn't any East Village. There were just a lot of blocks above the Lower East Side, some of them full of Ukrainians, a few Poles. The same buildings are still there, but the real estate people realized you could charge more rent if it had a name, maybe a name that suggested Greenwich Village. Presto: the East Village. This is postmodern. Also, since nobody ever referred to those blocks as the East Village before these people who owned the buildings started doing it them-selves, you could say that it was self-referential."

"The paper circulates in other neighborhoods, too," Jeffrey said. "Although I can't claim the circulation is very large. Of course, all this is completely up to you, Mr. Tepper."

Tepper looked at Jeffrey Green for a while without saying anything. Then he said, "Why not?"

9. *Name in the News*

TEPPER WAS FLIPPING THROUGH SOME RATE CARDS THAT had just come in—pausing now and then to study the attributes of a mailing list made up of "24,000 cash and charge customers of exclusive men's shop" or "16,000 executives in chemical management"—when he heard from the door, "Can I interrupt you for a moment, Murray?" Glancing at his watch as he looked up, Tepper saw that it was eleven-fifteen. Arnie Sarnow was pretty much on time.

"Why not, Arnie," he said. "Come in."

"What about lettuce dryers?" Arnie said, without bothering with the usual morning greetings.

"Lettuce dryers?" Tepper repeated. "You're thinking that Barney Mittgin can sell his map-pillows with a list of people who have sent away for lettuce dryers?"

"What? Oh, no," Arnie said. "This isn't about Barney Mittgin."

"Oh, sorry. I misunderstood," Tepper said. "Now that I think of it, Barney Mittgin was selling a lettuce dryer for a while. It could be used to spin the lettuce dry, but it also converted into something that could be used to play roulette, or maybe it was spin the bottle. I suppose that's what made me think we were talking about Barney Mittgin. That and our previous conversation about the airplane pillow."

"Oh, no, I was talking about the magic button," Arnie said. "The one we've talked about before."

Tepper and Arnie Sarnow had indeed talked often about what Arnie called the magic button—so often, in fact, that Tepper was beginning to regret having brought up the subject in the first place. Their first magic-button conversation had taken place not long after Arnie Sarnow came to work for Worldwide Lists. Tepper was telling Arnie how in the old days there were a couple of lists—the customer list of a wallet company, for instance, and the subscription list of a health magazine—that seemed to work for selling a broad variety of products. Arnie had been struck with the possibility of finding a single item that, probably for reasons nobody understood, marked true consumers—people who might not have any other common interest or even a common income bracket but did have in common an insatiable itch to respond to the offers they received through the mail. He believed that someone who figured out what that item was could, simply by building a list of people who had bought it, sell absolutely anything—portable saunas and life insurance and matched luggage and attaché cases that turned into foldout computer tables.

"It would be like having a magic button," Arnie often said. "You press it, and money comes out." Fairly regularly, Arnie would get a strong hunch about one item or another. If he could come by a list that was limited to that item alone—a list of people who had bought lettuce dryers, for instance, instead of a kitchen supply list that included people who had bought lettuce dryers—he'd sometimes persuade Tepper or Howard Gordon to approve what was called in the trade a Taunton test. For a good deal of money, a company called Taunton Direct Mails would do an accelerated test of a list, using e-mail and phone banks to get results that would have taken weeks or months by ordinary mail.

"Lettuce dryers," Tepper repeated. "What was it last time we talked—gardening gloves?"

"Adjustable shower heads," Arnie said. "The time before that was gardening gloves. High-quality gardening gloves. I think this would be better than either one of those. For one thing, I think the magazine would be stronger."

"Magazine?"

"Once we got a start on the list, we'd use it to send out a subscription pitch for a new magazine called *Spin: The Magazine of Salad Drying*. Then we'd have that subscription list to build on, but also we could sell ads for a fortune."

"There's enough to write about lettuce drying to have a magazine?" Tepper asked.

"I think you can hire people for that," Arnie said. "They've got magazines for everything now, Murray. There are magazines about nothing but ice-cream scoops. Putting out magazines for ferret owners is a competitive field."

"Well, that's an interesting idea—lettuce dryers," Tepper said. While he was trying to think of something more specific to say about lettuce dryers, Howard Gordon came into the office in what was, for him, a state of excitement.

"Did you ever hear of a newspaper called the East Village *Rag*?" he said, waving a newspaper that he held in his hand. "What kind of name is that for a newspaper anyway?"

"It's postmodern," Tepper said. "But not in a way that's easy to explain."

Howard Gordon looked puzzled for a moment, and then tossed the newspaper onto Tepper's desk. The paper was opened to the fourth page, which had a headline right across the top: QUIET WISDOM IN A CHEVY MALIBU. The byline was Jeffrey Green's. There was a picture of Murray Tepper, seen through the window of the driver's side, reading a newspaper. A story below the picture took up the rest of the page:

Murray Tepper is always in a legal spot. On Sundays, his dark blue Chevrolet Malibu is often parked in front of Russ & Daughters appetizing store on Houston Street. During the week, it can sometimes be found on one of the side streets near the theater district or on the Upper East Side. When someone slows down and asks if Mr. Tepper is going out, he always says no. Murray Tepper is not going out until he's good and ready.

Nobody knows why Murray Tepper is there. He doesn't seem to have any business to conduct in the neighborhood. He doesn't leave his car. When asked recently what he was doing parked on Houston Street, in front of Russ & Daughters, he said, "I was reading the paper."

Is Murray Tepper one of those people who is mad as hell and isn't taking it anymore? If so, he doesn't show it. Mr. Tepper gives the impression of a very even-tempered man. He's a mailing-list broker by trade—a partner in Worldwide Lists, which has offices in the West Twenties. Is he trying to escape from a messy situation at home? Apparently not. He says he's a happily married man. He lives with his wife, a watercolorist, in an apartment on West End Avenue. He has a married daughter and one grandson.

Although he is uniformly courteous, he doesn't offer any clues as to his motives. When he was asked last Sunday why he was parked on Houston Street without any apparent business in the neighborhood, he said, "I've got another twenty minutes on the meter."

Mr. Tepper has been subject to some harsh language now and then by people who want his parking spot, but other people find his presence a comfort. Apparently, Murray Tepper approaches some of life's other problems with the directness he employs in parking, and talking to him can be a soothing experience. One employee of Russ & Daughters, Irving Saper of Brooklyn, said, "I spent some time in there with him not long ago, and I've never felt better in my life. I wouldn't be surprised if pretty soon you're going to find a line of people waiting to get into that car."

The possibility that Mr. Tepper may be gifted with special insights was also raised by one of his clients, Barney Mittgin, of BarnEsther Novelties, a firm in Roslyn, Long Island. In an interview in the outer office of Worldwide Lists, Mr. Mittgin said, "Murray Tepper has some way of seeing things that other people can't see. He sees the connective tissue of our society. People in the industry call him Magic Touch Tepper."

But Mr. Tepper apparently can't see into the future, at least when it comes to parking. Asked by a reporter if he would be in front of Russ & Daughters again next Sunday, he replied, "If I can find a spot."

Tepper put the newspaper down. "'Connective tissue of our society?'" he said. "When did Barney Mittgin start talking like that?"

"I think his wife has been taking him to some of these adult education lectures at the Ninety-second Street Y," Arnie said.

"Apparently, this reporter came over here Monday or Tuesday and we were both gone," Gordon said. "And he got to talking to Mittgin in the outer office—not realizing he was interviewing a schmuck."

There was silence. Gordon and Arnie seemed to be waiting for Murray Tepper to say something about the *Rag* article beyond his observation about Barney Mittgin's language, but Tepper didn't speak. Finally, Gordon said, "Well, I suppose this sort of thing could bring in some business."

"I suppose," Tepper said.

There was more silence. Then, as Gordon and Arnie were about to leave, Tepper said, "Howard?"

"Yes, Murray," Gordon said.

"I wouldn't have thought you were a reader of the East Village *Rag*," Tepper said. "Is there something I've missed about you all these years?"

"My niece sent it to me," Gordon said. "She lives on Rivington Street. I don't know if that's included in what they call the East Village. We still call it the Lower East Side. You don't even want to know what she paid for her apartment. A co-op. A co-op on Rivington Street! I told her that her great-grandparents worked sixteen hours a day just to get out of Rivington Street.

What was cooperative about those buildings when they lived in them was the bathroom. Now whatever miserable cold-water flat my grandparents lived in has probably been made into a co-op. For all we know, that may be her co-op. She may be paying thousands to live in the place her great-grandparents worked themselves to death so their children wouldn't have to live in. What a city."

10. *Sushi*

THE JAPANESE WAITRESS, DRESSED IN KIMONO AND SAN-
dals, shuffled over, put a pot of tea on their table, and asked, in
heavily accented English, if they were ready to order.

"The regular sushi special," Jack said to the waitress. "And
make that medium well."

"Mee-dyum wher-ah?" the waitress said, looking puzzled.

"That means no pink showing in the center," Jack said.

Tepper waved his index finger in Jack's direction—not far
from the gesture he used sometimes when people asked him if
he was going out—and shook his head, indicating to the waitress
that she needn't pay any attention to what Jack was saying. "Just
bring us two regular sushi specials and two Kirin beers, please,"
Tepper said.

Jack shrugged. "Okay, get trichinosis, see if I care," he said.

"She must be new," Tepper said, after the waitress had left
the table. "The manager told me that the waitresses call you the
medium well man."

"So, you found any decent spots lately or are you still spending a lot of time circling around the block?" Jack said.

"Oh no, I'm finding some spots," Tepper said. "I really can't
complain."

Jack was silent for some time, as he busied himself pouring both of them some tea. The restaurant was just about full, and at most tables the conversation was animated. At three tables, one of the customers in a group of three or four was talking on a cell phone, and gradually it dawned on Tepper that, judging from their expressions and precisely when they spoke, two of them seemed to be talking to each other. Could that be? Wouldn't the one who called just walk over to the table of the person he wanted to talk to rather than place a call? But maybe he didn't realize the person he had called was eating at the same restaurant, just twenty feet away.

Finally, Jack said, "Do you remember when we ran into those two Vassar girls wandering around Washington Square, and we didn't think they'd be very impressed if we said we were just two schlemiels going to NYU on the ass end of the G.I. Bill so we told them we went to West Point? I called you Captain, and you kept saying, 'As you were, Sergeant Major.' Remember that? You couldn't get enough of that phrase: 'As you were, Sergeant Major.'"

"No, I don't remember that, Jack," Tepper said. "We kept *hoping* we'd find two Vassar girls wandering around Washington Square, but we never did."

"That's right," Jack said. "I was just testing you, in case you were an impostor. If you turned out to be an impostor, then when people said to me, 'Hey, what's this I hear about your friend Murray Tepper parking his car for pleasure? He used to be such a levelheaded guy. What does he have—some trouble with his hormones, or something?' I'd say, 'That's not Murray Tepper—that's a man who claims to be Murray Tepper. Murray Tepper has better things to do than park in someone else's parking spot. No, that man is an impostor: I tripped him up with a shrewd question on Vassar girls. I figure he's a Russian spy—an agent in place, a mole. The Russians want a capitalist economy over there, and they're trying to steal some of our business secrets. So they sent someone to pretend to be Murray Tepper long enough to steal a lot of inside dope on how to sell people tchotchkes through the mail.' But I didn't trip you up, because you correctly pointed out that the Vassar girls existed only in the fevered, lustful imagination of my youth. So what now?"

"Now we'll have some sushi, and you'll go back to your office and I'll go back to my office," Tepper said. "And every now and then you'll still think of the Vassar girls."

"No, I mean what do I tell them?" Jack said. "When people ask me about it, and I can't claim that you're an impostor, what do I tell them?"

"I sort of like the Russian spy explanation," Tepper said. "Maybe you could forget that you didn't trip me up with the Vassar girls story."

"Do you know what your son-in-law now thinks this is all about?"

"I don't, but you do," Tepper said.

"That's right. He tells Linda and Linda tells Ruth and Ruth doesn't tell you, because she's giving you some space. She tells me. It doesn't affect my space. Richard's latest theory, you might be pleased to hear, is that you're acting out your anger."

"What am I angry about?" Tepper asked. "Am I angry that my daughter married someone who talks like that?"

"He's not sure," Jack said. "He's working on it. He thinks you may be angry because you're getting on in years and you haven't made a real pile. Or, he tells Ruth, you may be angry because you realize that it's really not very important how many people buy which tchotchke through the mail—he apparently doesn't realize that information about this business is something the Russians would kill to get their hands on—and you therefore think that your life has been meaningless. Or you may be angry because of all the injustice and suffering and hypocrisy in the world. He thought for a while that you may be angry because they moved the Dodgers to Los Angeles, but after our little chat on Seventy-eighth Street I reminded Ruth that I was the one who was angry when they moved the Dodgers to Los Angeles. The bastards!"

Tepper just nodded. The waitress brought their sushi—pausing to gesture toward Jack and giggle and say, "you mee-dyum wher-ah man"—and they began eating.

"Or you're trying to prove something to yourself," Jack went on. "That's another one of his theories. You feel you sort of caved in when you put your car in a parking garage and quit looking for a spot that was good for tomorrow, like some nut looking for buried treasure in the desert. So you park, to prove to yourself that you can find a spot."

"That was alternate-side parking," Tepper said. "This is mostly meters."

"Listen, Murray," Jack said, after a while. "I know you think your son-in-law has some mushy ideas, but all this isn't that you're angry about something, is it? I mean, you don't *act* angry. But he's right that there are a lot of serious things in the world that could get a person pissed off."

Tepper just nodded, as he dipped a piece of tuna sushi into the soy sauce.

"Murray," Jack said. "Ruth and I talked about whether maybe

you should see somebody about this. A doctor or something. Some counseling. I mean, sure, everybody needs a hobby, but this. . . . Well, anyway, I actually know a guy, if you decided you might want to do that. He's more like a counselor. No couch or anything like that. He's got an office on East Sixty-eighth Street."

Tepper finished his tuna sushi, and reached for a piece of shrimp sushi. He started on the shrimp without saying anything.

"So, what do you think?" Jack finally said.

"About Sixty-eighth Street?"

"Well, yes."

"Mostly No Parking Eight-to-Six Monday through Friday there," Tepper said.

"What?"

"East Sixty-eighth Street. Mostly No Parking Eight-to-Six Monday through Friday. Or even No Standing Seven A.M. to Seven P.M."

"You're just putting me on, right?" Jack said.

"You could go look at the signs," Tepper said. "It's always been a hard street to park on. Because of the crosstown buses, I think. Or at least that's what they'd claim. I mean, the alternate-side regulations are supposedly for street cleaning, or at least that's what they claim. But who really knows?"

"No, that's not what I mean," Jack said. "I mean you're just trying to string me along when you answer the question about counseling by telling me what the parking situation is in front of the office. The way you told me the other night that Times Square was No Parking Anytime when I said I might go park there. That's a joke, right?"

"Some people take parking very seriously, Jack," Tepper said.

11. *Elevator Music*

TEPPER WAS PARKED IN FRONT OF RUSS & DAUGHTERS, eating a herring-salad-on-bagel sandwich that Irving Saper had been kind enough to bring along when he came out with a copy of the article in the East Village *Rag* for Tepper to autograph. It was about ten-thirty, Sunday morning. Tepper had just had a small scene with a man who was driving a Dodge station wagon with New Jersey plates. When Tepper waved the Dodge on, employing the sort of motion someone might use to help along the water in a bathtub that had a slow drain, the driver hadn't moved. Instead, he had rolled down the window and shouted, "This isn't the public reading room, buddy. This is a street!" Then he'd turned to a woman sitting in the passenger seat next to him and said, still shouting, "He thinks this is a public reading room. This guy thinks this is a public reading room. This is not a public reading room." Tepper had ignored him, and, finally, the Dodge station wagon had pulled away.

Tepper was involved in reading a long story about someone who had become rich and famous in California by preaching that he was a mere container for an eleven-thousand-year-old spirit named Kravoo. The container's followers had bought him many cars. He was a regular on television talk shows. His book was on the bestseller list. Now he was being challenged by a former disciple who claimed that she was inhabited by a spirit who was fourteen thousand years old, three thousand years older than Kravoo—that her spirit, in other words, had the wisdom that comes with more life experience. The man who was Kravoo's container was fighting back. He said that he knew the spirit inhabiting his former disciple and that it was a spirit who was only four thousand years old. "In effect, we're talking about a kid here," he had said. "Just a kid."

There was a knock on the passenger-side window. A man was at the window saying, "Mr. Tepper? Murray Tepper?" He formed the words in an exaggerated way, presumably in case Tepper could not hear him through the glass and might want to read his lips. Tepper had never seen the man before. He was a thin man, with rimless glasses. He was dressed in a suit and tie, an unusual outfit on Houston Street on Sunday morning. Even though he had approached a complete stranger, his looks and manner were rather diffident. Tepper rolled the window down, so he could hear the man better.

"My name is Edwin Milledge," the man said. "Are you the Mr. Tepper who goes and parks sometimes?"

"My name is Tepper, and I'm parked here. It's metered parking nine to seven, *including* Sundays."

Milledge smiled. "You're the right Mr. Tepper, all right," he said.

"How do you know me?" Tepper asked, although he thought he already knew the answer.

"I read about you in the East Village *Rag*, and it said you might be back here today—if you could find a spot. I wonder if I could talk to you for a few minutes."

"Why not?" Tepper said, swinging open the passenger-side door. "Have a seat."

Edwin Milledge came in and settled in the front seat and didn't say anything for a while. Then he said, "You see, I really hate the canned music in the elevators. I truly hate it."

"There's always something," Tepper said.

"It's not that I don't like music. In fact, it's quite the opposite. I love music. That's why I subscribe to the East Village *Rag*: They often have notices of New Music concerts that other papers don't mention. My whole life is music, really, except for my job and my family. I've played the cello since I was a child. At one time I actually thought of trying for a career as a classical cellist, although in my heart I knew I wasn't that good. But I love it. I play in a string quartet. I practice every evening."

"Do you mind if I ask you a question?" Tepper said.

"No, of course not."

"Are you also interested in mathematics?"

"Why, yes. Yes I am. My job actually has to do with mathematics. I work for a firm that does research and development, mostly for telephone companies. My degree is in mathematics."

"Interesting, interesting," Tepper said. "There's a theory, as you may know, that there's a connection between music and mathematics—the same part of the brain, or something like that. Apparently, people who are good at music are often good at mathematics, and vice versa. I've been testing the theory a little—trying to sell Brahms CDs to people who'd sent away for books on mathematics, that sort of thing. How about chess?"

"I'm afraid I don't understand," Milledge said.

"Do you play chess?"

"Yes, I'm a fairly serious player."

"Interesting, interesting. I don't suppose you're interested in exotic sorts of foods, too?"

"No, I'm afraid not," Milledge said. "I'm afraid I'm what they used to call strictly a meat-and-potatoes man."

"Well, that doesn't fit," Tepper said. "There was a theory that math and music and exotic eating often all went together."

"Well, I might be an exception," Milledge said helpfully. "I do like sardines now and then, but I don't suppose that would be considered strictly exotic."

"Oh, that's all right. Don't eat sardines on my account," Tepper said. "I was just curious. I assume you do not own a lettuce dryer."

"No, no lettuce dryer."

"Well, I didn't mean to interrupt you," Tepper said. "You were talking about the music in elevators."

"The building I work in has music in the elevators," Milledge said. "I've complained to my boss, but he says, quite correctly, that our company doesn't own the building. We only have one floor. I've talked to the people who manage the building, but they don't seem interested. I tried circulating a petition among the people who work in the building, but they don't seem interested either. I try to explain to them that it's not the music that's played that offends me, although it's not the sort of music I like, of course. It's the idea of music as background, what someone once called aural wallpaper. I hate that."

"Well, as I said, there's always something."

"The thing is," Milledge went on, "I'm thinking very seriously about taking extreme steps." As he said that, Milledge seemed to square his shoulders and sit more erectly in the front seat.

Tepper nodded his head slowly. "What sort of extreme steps?" he asked.

"Oh, there wouldn't be any violence, of course," Milledge said. "I once heard that some years ago some people who worked for a magazine objected to canned music in the elevator. A group of them would wait until they got to their floor, and then simply stand in the door, refusing to leave until the piece they were listening to was over."

"But I take it you don't have a group of people."

"No, there's just me. Oh, possibly Miss Murtaugh, from collating."

"Another musician?"

Milledge nodded. "She plays the viola. She's quite good, really. But Miss Murtaugh and I alone obviously couldn't make an impact by refusing to leave, like those magazine people. So I was thinking about shorting out the system. Not the entire elevator system—just the part that controls the music. I think I can make the distinction easily enough. I'm quite good at electrical things."

Tepper nodded. "If I may ask, Mr. Milledge," he said. "Do you find that other musicians of your acquaintance are also good at electrical things?"

Milledge considered the question for a moment. "Not that I've noticed," he said.

"If I may ask one other question," Tepper said. "Why, exactly, are you telling me this? I don't mean that it isn't interesting. I do find it interesting. But why particularly me?"

"Because reading about you in that article has given me courage," Milledge said. "You've inspired me. You face questions head-on. Why are you parked here today?"

"Because it's a legal spot—as long as you've put a quarter in the meter, of course," Tepper said.

"Exactly!" Milledge said. "And do you intend to leave?"

"No, I'm not going out," Tepper said.

"Exactly!" Milledge reached over and shook Tepper's hand vigorously. "Exactly!" he nearly shouted. "Exactly!"

There was a knock on the window. During his conversation with Milledge, Tepper suddenly realized, two or three other people had gathered on the sidewalk next to the car. In other words, people were waiting in line to talk to him.

12.   *Survey Results*

"WHAT DO YOU MEAN, 'SIT DOWN THERE?'" SHANAHAN
said to Teresa. He was standing in the outer office of the mayor's
suite, holding his laptop computer. He had already successfully
completed the iris check.

"Just sit down there," Teresa repeated, pointing to an odd-
looking chair. "Put your little computer over here by my desk,
just in case whatever that thing's got in it turns computer programs into raspberry Jell-O, and sit down."

The chair was made of a dark gray material that appeared
to be some sort of composite of ash or soot. It looked rather
forbidding—hard material, straight edges. Extending from one
side was an adjustable attachment that looked as if it swung in to
provide a sort of chin rest for whoever was sitting in the chair.
The chair had dials.

"I actually heard about this, and I thought it was a joke,"
Shanahan said.

"It's no joke," Teresa said, picking up a four-color brochure.
"It is, in fact, a Body Orifice Security Scanner, also known as
a BOSS." She started reading from the brochure: "The low-
intensity magnetic fields pose no danger to people with heart
pacemakers or pregnant women. No X rays are used, so staff and

inmates are never subjected to . . ." She stopped. The light on her desk was flashing. "The mayor will see you now," she said to Shanahan.

Shanahan started to walk toward the mayor's office, but Teresa put her hand on his arm. "As soon as you sit in the chair—the Body Orifice Security Scanner," she said. He put his laptop computer next to Teresa's desk, walked over to the BOSS, and sat down, lowering himself with some delicacy, like a fraternity pledge who had just undergone some brutal paddling. There was no sound. "You did fine," Teresa said, as she signaled him to stand up. "I can't guarantee that there's nothing in your body orifices, but if there is something it's not dangerous to others."

The mayor was actually sitting behind his desk, going through some papers. "Carmody's getting ready," he said, when he saw Shanahan. "I hear from somebody at the Players club that Maxie Allen never shows up there for lunch anymore. He's too busy working on songs with that clown Carmody."

"I hear the same thing," Shanahan said. "The word is that Carmody's going to run."

"I'll be going to Phoenix for this mayors' conference in about a week," Ducavelli said. "I figure by the time I get back from there we'll be seeing our friend Mr. Carmody around town a little more."

"Sounds about right," Shanahan said. "Unless he can't get the lyrics memorized by then."

"What's the latest we've got on a head-to-head?" Ducavelli said.

Shanahan put his laptop on the mayor's conference table, tapped a few keys, and said, "The latest is a five-hundred-voter phone survey we did a month ago. You win fifty-six to forty-four in a straight head-to-head. If the Reverend Alonzo Butler runs, as he threatens to do now and then when the police mistake an ice-cream cone or key ring in the hand of a black man as a gun and start firing away, he would pull about equally from you and Carmody."

"Alonzo Butler is a hypocrite and false leader," the mayor said. "Anybody who preaches in Harlem and lives in Yonkers is a coward who is obviously trying to get out of the range of my authority so he won't find a methadone treatment center next door to his house, which is what he deserves to find, and what he *will* find if I can ever persuade that wimp mayor of Yonkers that granting a lawful request from a fellow mayor is a matter of common courtesy. Yes, Alonzo Butler is an obviously and irredeemably corrupt and degraded human being. That's the long and short of it."

"Be that as it may," Shanahan said, "he pulls about equally from you and the Wacko, so you still lead the Wacko by roughly twelve points."

"The man's a clown," Ducavelli said, almost to himself. "A disgrace." The mayor sat staring into the middle distance for a while, occasionally muttering a word like "fool" or "degenerate," like a motor that is basically about out of fuel but is still coughing a bit irregularly. Then, after a while, he looked at Mike Shanahan as if Shanahan had just come into the office. "You were going to give me some survey results on parking, Mike," he said. "Parking's the thing. Bedrock!"

Shanahan tapped again at his computer. "The parking situation is pretty simple, Mayor," he said. "When you try to crack down on United Nations diplomats, your numbers go up; when you try to crack down on ordinary citizens for, say, double parking, your numbers go down." A few months before, the mayor had decided, rather abruptly, that double-parking your car while waiting behind the wheel, maybe even with the motor running, was essentially the same as double-parking your car, locking it, and leaving. He had ordered a crackdown.

"Double parkers are criminals," the mayor said.

"Well, I won't argue the legalities, Mayor, but what they consider themselves, which turns out to be what's important in their view of your crackdown on double parking, is maybe miscreants at worst and maybe even people waiting for their wives to get out of a store so they can drive home to Queens."

"A double-parked car is a call to lawlessness," the mayor said. "It's like a sign inviting in the forces of disorder."

"Your campaign against the Ukrainians was one of the most popular things you've ever done," Shanahan continued, deciding that there was no point in continuing a discussion of double parking with Mayor Ducavelli. "Although I say that as one who is opposed to an actual declaration of war. According to our data, the phrase 'scofflaws in striped pants' was the phrase you used that voters liked best of any phrase associated with you all year. I should say that there aren't many Ukrainian voters. Those Ukrainians who used to live in what they're now calling the East Village seem to have been replaced by boutiques, and the immigrants from around Kiev who live in Brooklyn are actually Jews who have good reason not to leap to their feet when the Ukrainian national anthem is played. So, even though our survey shows that sticking it to the diplomats is generally good politics, it also shows that it depends on which diplomats you stick it to. If the main scofflaws among diplomats were the Israelis or the Irish or the Italians, you might come out ahead by letting bygones be bygones."

Toward the end of that report, the mayor had seemed to tune out. He was again staring out at nothing particular, muttering. "Buffoon," he said after a while. And then, "Fool." And then, "Poltroon."

13. *A Mittgin Morning*

TEPPER THOUGHT OF IT AS HIS BARNEY MITTGIN MORN-
ing. He'd have time to do some other business, of course. In fact,
he had a consultation scheduled with the circulation people
planning the charter subscription drive for one of those new
magazines aimed at women over fifty—a magazine that was tentatively called *Laughlines,* although its circulation people, all
of them male, generally referred to it among themselves as
Cellulite. He was also meeting with some people from the campaign committee of a young man who was running for Congress
in Westchester County as a pro-choice free-market anti-tax
gun-control pro-NATO Republican reformer. The committee,
frustrated in its attempts to encompass the candidate's natural
constituency through the lists available from conventional
political sources, thought that Tepper might be able to come up
with something. Tepper also had some other odds and ends to
do. He was planning to pick some doctors' lists to test for a sort
of real estate mutual fund—for reasons he couldn't explain, he
had the strong feeling that allergists were going to be a strong
market—and if he had time he might do a little research on lettuce dryers, just to have something to report to Arnie Sarnow
when the subject of the magic list came up. But he still thought of

the morning as the morning Barney Mittgin was coming by Worldwide Lists to demonstrate once again what a schmuck he was.

Mittgin showed up at nine-thirty. He was a man who had put on weight in a way that called to mind a sausage that had been filled at a rate that was a bit too much for its casing—particularly for some weak sections that bulged out grotesquely from the whole. He often got out of breath and red in the face. Tepper noticed that Mittgin vaguely resembled the fat man on West Fifty-seventh Street who had kept shouting, "Ya jerky bastard, ya."

"Well, it's the famous Murray Tepper," Mittgin said, when he walked into the office and took the seat next to Tepper's desk. The chair had been vacated ten or fifteen minutes before by Arnie Sarnow, who had dropped in just long enough to report that Mittgin, in a foul state about the failure of Worldwide Lists to come up with a satisfactorily imaginative approach to selling his device for sleeping on airplanes and finding your way around airports, had insisted on spending some time with Murray Tepper himself.

Tepper shrugged. "Not overwhelmingly famous," he said.

"Hope this isn't pushing you, Touch, me coming in without much warning," Mittgin said, as he settled in.

"No problem, Barney," Tepper said. "I've got a meeting with some political campaign people in a while, but I think we've got enough time."

Mittgin smiled. "Ah, the political people want to talk to the man with the magic touch—the man who found the car-cleaner list."

"Barney, I didn't have anything to do with the car-cleaner list. You've got that mixed up." Tepper felt constrained to make the denial even though he didn't have any illusions that it would do much good. Once Mittgin got an idea in his head, it couldn't be dislodged by constant bombardment of contradictory facts. Tepper had not, in fact, had anything to do with finding the car-cleaner list, although he had always been fascinated by its effectiveness. In the sixties, a list broker working for the Republican National Committee must have been testing what amounted to wild-card lists, among them a list of people who had sent away for a chemically treated cloth that was effective for "washing" a car without the use of water. As a list for Republican fund-raising it turned out to be second in effectiveness only to a list of people who had sent away for copies of *Six Crises* by Richard M. Nixon. The Democrats in the trade explained the success of the car-cleaner list with no trouble at all: they said that the average Republican donor was not only abnormally interested in maintaining his property but too stiff to get wet while doing it. But Tepper had heard that the car-cleaner list also worked for the Democratic National Committee. He had pondered for years what exterior car maintenance and willingness to donate money to politicians could possibly have in common. The connection never came.

"You've got the touch, Murray," Mittgin said, and then sat smiling at him as if he expected Tepper to demonstrate his magic touch right there. "You're a modest man, but you've got the touch. Don't forget the No list."

Tepper nodded. The No list. The No was one of his all right, although he didn't consider it anything more than the sort of connection he made dozens of times a week. The No list was the list of people who had sent back sweepstakes offers marked "No"—exercising the option to have their name remain in the running for a prize but declining the subscription or set of books or travel offer the sweepstakes was designed to sell. The No option had to be included by law, but the people who ran sweep-stakes would have included it anyway. They had found that offer-ing the option to say no increased the percentage of people who said yes—presumably because the extra split second people kept the mailing in their hand to think about the decision led to a tiny but significant number of them deciding to take out the sub-scription after all.

For years nobody had found a use for the No list, beyond some relatively minor mailings for puzzle and game magazines. It just sat there, tantalizing people in the trade who considered any unused list of names arable land lying fallow. The people on the No list had demonstrated that they were willing to deal through the mails. They had demonstrated that they were willing to risk a first-class stamp for a fantastically long shot at winning a new cabin cruiser or $25,000 for ten years. The solution that Tepper thought of was so simple that it almost didn't qualify as a connection. A number of states were then looking for ways to broaden their state lotteries, and a couple of them were actually considering mailings—a play-by-mail lottery. They had the state motor vehicles registration lists at their disposal, but those were too broad. By taking the No list and slicing it into states on a computer, Tepper provided the state lotteries with lists of hard-core long-shot something-for-nothing people. He was known in the business for a while as the man who found a use for the No list, but Tepper himself considered it a flash in the pan.

Not Barney Mittgin. He was one of those people who insisted on covering people with praise for accomplishments they either hadn't had anything to do with or knew to be of no particular consequence. At least that's the way he treated Tepper. Since Tepper avoided Mittgin outside the absolute necessities of their business dealings, he had no way of knowing whether everyone else got the same treatment. Sometimes, though, he could imagine Mittgin arriving home every evening and gushing over something his wife had, for good reason, considered routine at best. "No wonder everyone describes you as a gourmet cook," he'd say at dinner. "This turkey is magnificent. A triumph."

"It's one of those frozen dinners, Barney," Mittgin's unfortunate wife would say. "I just thawed it out. Gourmets don't thaw."

"When I think of the blessing I've been given to have such a wife—a genuine gourmet cook . . ."

The other side of Mittgin's misplaced admiration was the belief that people he had not admitted into his pantheon of heroes were absolutely incompetent—which is what he had decided about Arnie Sarnow. "He's a nice boy, Murray, but he doesn't have the touch," Mittgin said.

"I thought Arnie did pretty well testing subscription lists from computer-repair magazines," Tepper said.

Mittgin shook his head. "He doesn't have the touch, Murray. Remember when you found the accountants list for the discount designer jeans? Other people might have put together accountants and discount, but accountants and designer jeans—that's you, Murray. That's the magic touch."

"I think Arnie must have handled that one, Barney. I didn't do any designer jeans account."

"It took someone who knew what makes this country tick to make that connection, Murray," Mittgin went on, as if Tepper hadn't spoken. "It took someone with the magic touch."

"Maybe it's the product, Barney," Tepper said, even though he knew it would do no good. "Maybe not that many people feel the need for a sleep doughnut with airport maps on it."

"It's not the product, Murray. I've got a hundred and fifty gross of the product to move. It can't be the product."

14.   *Dinner*

MURRAY TEPPER COULD TELL THAT RUTH WAS ABOUT TO introduce an important subject by the way she said his name before she began. They were sitting at the dinner table in their apartment on the West Side, in the same dining room they had eaten in for twenty-five years. They were having roast chicken. Ruth often started sentences with his name—she had, in fact, just said, "Murray, could you pass the salt, please?"—but this was a different tone from the one she used for getting the salt or for asking some routine question, like "Murray, do you want this shirt to go to the laundry or what?" This was a more considered tone. The first syllable of his name was emphasized, and the two syllables were separated more firmly.

"Murray," she said. "What do you think about going back to England sometime this summer?"

Tepper was working on a chicken leg. His mouth was full of dark meat.

"Or maybe in September," Ruth said, before he could reply. "When the airline fares go down."

"England's a nice little country," he said.

Ruth considered that answer for a moment. It was probably

not a description of the United Kingdom that the British ambassador would go for, but, coming from Murray, it seemed enthusiastic enough to warrant pursuit of the subject. Murray had, in fact, always seemed to enjoy England. From time to time, they had even talked about retiring there one day, in one of those pretty, peaceful villages in the West, just a few fields in from the sea. Calling England "a nice little country" wasn't necessarily meant in a condescending way. It wasn't unusual for Murray to describe a country in terms of its geographic size. She had heard him refer to France once as "a nice middle-sized country." When the subject of Canada came up, he was likely to say, "Very big. Very, very big."

"We could go to the seashore in the West of England," Ruth said. "I'd love to do some watercolors there—Devon, Cornwall. You told me once that my seascapes were your favorites."

"It's true," Tepper said. "That's partly because I particularly like your pictures when they have a lot of blue in them. Your blue is spectacular, Ruth. Truly spectacular. Nobody's blue is like your blue."

When Tepper met the woman who was to be his wife, just after the war, she was studying art full-time. She had come to New York hoping to be a painter. Until Linda was born, Ruth had worked as an illustrator. She'd also done some graphic design. Her true love, though, was working in watercolors. Ruth's style hadn't really changed much in all of those years. She still used mainly watercolors, and her subjects were still mostly landscapes and seascapes. Tepper preferred the seascapes, because of the blue, but he found all of Ruth's work soothing. When he read in the paper about an artist who was drawing attention for some avant-garde departure, he sometimes wondered how he would respond if he arrived home one evening to find Ruth intently pasting turkey feathers and bits of alfalfa on a canvas that had been painted four shades of black. But when he returned from the office each evening and peeked into the room Ruth used as her studio—what had formerly been Linda's bedroom—he always saw, to his relief, that Ruth's style was unchanged. She painted what she had always painted—the rocks, the tumbledown fishing shacks, the blue water, the blue sky, sometimes a blue pickup truck.

"You don't have anything that would keep you here, do you?" Ruth asked.

"Keep me here?" Tepper said. "I can't think of anything that would keep me here. Like what?"

"Oh, you know. Maybe some project at the office, or maybe Howard wants to take off in September, or some activity or something?"

"Some activity?" Tepper asked.

Ruth didn't say anything for a while. Then she said, "Murray"—it was the serious "Murray"—"if we go to England, would you still want to . . . you know . . . read the paper in the car?"

"You mean go out parking in the evenings?" Tepper asked.

"Well, yes," Ruth said.

"The parking situation might be completely different over there," Tepper said. "I didn't really study it when we were there before. Especially in a little seaside town in Devon or Cornwall it might be different. I can't believe they have alternate-side parking, the way we do, for instance. Although, I don't know. It's for street cleaning, alternate-side parking, and the English are very interested in being tidy. You've got to do that when it's a little country. Otherwise, the stuff really piles up."

"You mean you do it here because of something about the parking situation?" she asked.

"Not exactly," Tepper said.

Ruth continued eating her chicken in silence. Finally, she said, "Murray, I'm not sure whether all that meant you would want to go parking in the evenings in England or you wouldn't."

"Oh, I would never leave you alone in a hotel in a foreign country, Ruth," Tepper said.

Ruth smiled. "That's a nice thing to say, Murray," she said.

"I suppose you could come along," Tepper said, "if you weren't busy with your watercolors."

Ruth put down her fork. "Then, Murray, going out parking in the evenings doesn't have anything to do with me," she said. It was partly a question, partly a statement. "I mean, you didn't feel you just had to get out of the house, or anything like that."

"Of course not, Ruth," Tepper said. "I told you that before. It's just something I do."

Ruth nodded, as if reassuring herself. "I guess it's sort of a hobby. That's what I told Harriet. A hobby. An unusual hobby, but a hobby. Everybody's entitled to a hobby. And you never had a hobby, Murray. All these other men were doing carpentry and golf and coin collecting. Remember when Milt started building birdhouses? He filled their apartment with birdhouses. As if birds are going to go to an apartment building on West End Avenue and go up in the elevator and into the Davidsons' apartment and settle down in a birdhouse. So now you have a hobby, if that's what it is. You know what I thought at first, Murray—when you first started going?"

"What?"

"I thought: Maybe he's got a girl. Then I thought: Murray? Never! Then I thought: People at this age do funny things."

"That's what Howard Gordon was saying," Murray said. "At this age, people do funny things."

"Howard never did anything funny," Ruth said.

"He laughed once, but it was a long time ago."

"I don't think I ever thought it seriously—that you had a girlfriend. I don't think I would have thought it at all except for that word: parking. In Springfield, when I was a teenager, when girls talked over a date one of them had been on, the other one would ask, 'Did he try to park?' and that meant did he want to go someplace dark and lonely in a car and neck, or whatever."

"That's interesting," Tepper said. "You never told me about that. 'Did he try to park?' What kind of rules did you have?"

Ruth smiled. "Goodness. I haven't thought of that in years," she said. "Well, when the boy headed for one of those parking places—they were all well-known—and the girl didn't say something about having to get home, it was assumed that she was at least willing to do a little necking. And then, if the boy started in that direction and the girl really didn't want—"

"No, I mean the parking rules," Tepper said.

"Parking rules?"

"Yeah, you know: alternate-side parking? Meters?"

"I can't remember, Murray," Ruth said. "I really can't remember. That was a long time ago. Is it important?"

Murray shrugged. "I suppose I could write and ask," he said.

15.   *Office Hours*

IN FRONT OF RUSS & DAUGHTERS THAT SUNDAY, TEPPER hardly had time to begin his customary perusal of the *Sunday News* when the knocks on the passenger-side window began. What they interrupted was Tepper reading about himself. The *News* had run a short item on Tepper early in the week—apparently, the editors had been alerted by Jeffrey Green's story in the East Village *Rag*—and the Sunday newspaper carried a few letters on the subject. One of them concluded that Tepper was a New Yorker who had been driven over the edge by the stresses in the city, particularly the sales tax—a tax that the writer described, in some detail, as putting an unconstitutionally disproportionate burden on both the poor and the materialistic. Another maintained that Tepper's parking was a form of political theater: Murray Tepper was obviously protesting Mayor Ducavelli's insane insistence on enforcing obscure and petty laws, the form of protest being what labor people would call a work to rules action. There was a letter saying that this episode made you yearn for a mayor like Bill Carmody, and there was a letter saying that Tepper was obviously an agent of former mayor Bill Carmody, trying to undermine by deceitful means an effective mayor whom Carmody had not been able to defeat in a fair election. There was a letter explaining that Murray Tepper was simply trying to find inner peace but never would until he embraced Buddhism.

Around nine-thirty Irving Saper, the counterman, came out of the store to say hello and to report that, inspired by his conversation with Tepper, he had begun inventing again—a device for slicing salmon, actually, that made it possible even for an amateur at home to achieve slices so thin that someone looking through them could discern light and dark shapes. "Being able to read the *Times* I don't guarantee," Saper said. "I'm not kidding myself." By that time there were four people standing on the sidewalk next to the Chevrolet, waiting for an opportunity to slip into the passenger seat for a chat with Tepper, and Saper had to assure them that he was not trying to jump the line. "Just a little progress report," he assured a woman who stood holding the door handle, the way New Yorkers sometimes do to claim possession of a taxi while the previous passenger is paying.

Occasionally, someone would just stop for a moment at the driver's side to congratulate Tepper and wish him luck. "Listen, there's nobody can force you to get out of this spot," Tepper was told by a tough-looking man who identified himself as a cabdriver. "You know why?"

"It's one-hour meter parking from nine to seven, Sunday included, and I've got fifty-five minutes to go on the meter," Tepper said.

"Well, that too. But the real reason is that this is America. You're an American! Never forget that: you're an American." The cabdriver paused for a short inspection of Tepper, studying his face carefully. Then he said, "You are an American, aren't you? You look like an American."

"Yes, I'm an American," Tepper said.

"You've got to ask these days," the cabdriver said. "Half the cabbies in town can't speak enough English to get through the Midtown Tunnel. These foreign bastards are taking over. You were born here?"

Tepper nodded, and the cabdriver, after giving that some consideration, said he was going to do some shopping and then he'd join the line on the sidewalk.

Some of the people who sat in the passenger's seat of Tepper's Chevy Malibu had come to tell him about complaints they had against the city. They told tales of corrupt officials and obdurate bureaucrats. "So, after eight or ten telephone calls, I finally found the right person in the Pension Department," one man said. "And I explained to him what I needed. My late uncle worked part-time for the Weights and Measures Department years ago, and before I could get my aunt on Medicaid, I had to produce a letter from somebody in authority saying that my uncle did not have a pension from the city. And this person on the telephone said that the first step would be for me to give him my uncle's pension number. And I told him that the point of this call was that my uncle didn't have a pension, so how could he have a pension number? And he said that, whatever the point of the call, he'd need a pension number before he could look it up. Then, I'm afraid I used some harsh language, and he hung up."

"There's always something," Tepper said.

Many of the people who stepped into Tepper's car wanted to tell him about something in their lives that they found irritating or even infuriating. They said that they wanted to be able to respond in the way Tepper seemed to be responding to whatever it was that had driven him to park his car in a legal spot and refuse to leave. They often remarked on how calm he appeared despite how angry he must be. Like Edwin Milledge, the man who loved music and hated the music in elevators, they seemed to gain confidence as they told their stories to Tepper. Occasionally, he would nod, or say, "There's always something," or answer their questions about his own activities by saying that he was in a legal spot or that he wasn't going out. Tepper was amazed that a couple of newspaper articles could produce a stream of people seeking help and guidance and advice. He was also amazed that, even though he didn't say much at all to his visitors, almost all of the people who sat in the front seat of his Chevy seemed certain that he had been of great help to them.

At times, people would list the pros and cons of a decision they were faced with at work, while Tepper nodded or put in a few words about how he'd made his own decisions at Worldwide Lists—how he'd come up with the lists he'd tested on the way to establishing the link between left-wing politics and gourmet cooking, for instance, or the link between cosmetics for men and sports-car ownership.

Several people had problems with their bosses. One of the first people to join Tepper in the front seat that morning, an actuary in a large insurance company, said that he'd served the company loyally for many years but had the feeling he wasn't satisfying his boss, who never seemed to look him in the eye. Fifteen minutes later, a man who described himself as an insurance executive said that he was increasingly suspicious of a certain employee whose work was satisfactory but who didn't seem capable of looking him in the eye. Tepper couldn't help wondering whether the employee in question was the very man who'd been in his car. If so, was there some way to find the man, whose name Tepper didn't even know? He could see himself bringing the two of them together and saying, "All right. Get ready. One. Two. Three. Look!" What he said out loud, though, was "A lot of people are shy."

One man wanted to talk about his immediate superior in an import-export firm downtown. "He has the attention span of a flea," the man said. "When you talk to him, he's always saying, 'yeah, yeah, yeah,' as if he's taking in what you're saying, but he doesn't hear anything. And here's what's amazing about it: he's always talking about people who don't pay attention. He has these awful little aphorisms on the subject—'The wise man listens while the fool talks on' and things like that. He's such a hypocrite. Now that I think of it, maybe that's why he's always saying things like 'Some hear while others only listen' or 'Some listen while others only hear' or whatever it is. Because he knows he doesn't hear or listen. He just says 'yeah, yeah.' That's what we call him around the office—Yeah-yeah. I don't know if he's aware of that. How would he know? Even if you called him that to his face he wouldn't know because he doesn't hear a word you say. I guess you must have a boss something like that—maybe that's why you're out here."

"No," Tepper said. "I have a partner, and he's a nice man. I can't say that he's a lot of laughs, but he's a nice man."

"Yeah, I know what you mean," the man said. "They're all like that. Hypocrites! Listen, let me tell you something else this guy does. He's always talking about people with beady eyes. He'll say, 'He's one of those beady-eyed guys.' That's his whole way of describing somebody who's got to be watched, somebody untrustworthy—that the guy has beady eyes. And you ought to see *his* eyes! He's the beadiest-eyed guy I've ever seen in my entire life. He's got these little bitty beady eyes. Talk about beady eyes! Can you imagine! Here's this guy with eyes that look like something Indians'll sell you at a roadside stand—these little beads— and he's talking about beady-eyed guys! Can you imagine!"

"There's always something," Tepper said.

"Exactly," the man said. "That's why I admire you—not just because you have the guts to be out here parking, sticking it to that boss of yours, but because you understand."

"I don't actually have a boss. You're the one with the boss."

"Yeah, yeah. I know. You're an inspiration to us all."

Occasionally, Tepper found that his experience in the mailing-list business had given him some means to answer people's questions. One man came to complain about the little subscription cards that fall out of magazines. He was an older man, courteous in an almost old-fashioned way. He introduced himself formally—his name was Ralph M. Lockwood—and apologized a couple of times for intruding on Tepper.

"For a while I just fumed about those cards," he said. "I found them exceedingly irritating. Mrs. Lockwood and I are both neat—we can't abide clutter—and I found that anytime we spent an evening reading magazines the parlor was simply littered with these dreadful little cards. Why must they pester us with those cards?"

"Well, I happen to be in a similar trade, and the answer is that if the publisher of a magazine were looking for subscribers he would be looking for people who have demonstrated in some way that they're the sort of people who might read his magazine and there's no way to demonstrate that better than to actually be reading the magazine. So he has his perfect customer pool right there, and I suppose he just can't resist the temptation."

"I must confess something to you, Mr. Tepper," Lockwood said. "I heard a man on television talking about how, since the cards say that postage will be paid by the magazine, he simply sends in the cards to the people in charge of processing them—he said they're called circulation fulfillment departments and they're very dreary places to work—and puts cheerful little notes on them, like 'Keep up the good work, circulation fulfillment people.' Well, that gave me an idea, and now I send in hundreds of those cards. Actually, thousands. I collect them in the dentist's office and on airplanes and sometimes right there on the floor in front of magazine racks, where they've fallen out of the magazines while people were browsing. But I don't put cheerful little messages in them. I say, 'Littering is wicked.' I had one of those stamps made—the kind you don't even need an ink pad for. Mrs. Lockwood and I sit down after dinner every night and do about fifty. Then we sit in the parlor and read magazines."

Tepper spoke with one woman who wanted to explain to him that the only pure pleasure she got out of life was playing the lottery. From his selling of the No list, Tepper was quite familiar with the various state lotteries, and the lottery fan was delighted to be talking to someone with such broad knowledge. As she was comparing the lotteries of the New England states, he heard a commotion outside the car. Apparently, a man in a Pontiac had pulled alongside and asked if Tepper was going out. Lost in the lottery story, Tepper hadn't heard the question or the honk that preceded it. The man had grown angry, and the sight of a line waiting to talk to Tepper made him angrier still.

"Whadaya, holding office hours in there or something?" the man in the Pontiac shouted. "You handing out safe-sex kits or something?"

Tepper, without looking over, gave the man a backhand flick. The man began to shout, "Ya jerky bastard, ya! Ya jerky bastard, ya!" Tepper turned and looked at the man in the Pontiac. It was the same fat, red-faced man who had yelled at him a few weeks before from a sport-utility vehicle on West Fifty-seventh Street. He had changed cars, but he was still yelling the same thing: "Ya jerky bastard, ya."

"Hey, watch your mouth, fella," the cabdriver who had come to tell Tepper about being an American said. "You looking for a fat lip, or what?"

"Mind your own business, you spic bastard!" the fat man said.

"Spic! Who you calling a spic! I'm an American, you dago scumbag!"

The cabdriver, after asking the woman in front of him to hold his place in line, moved closer to the Pontiac. The fat man seemed about ready to get out and confront the cabdriver. Several other people who had been standing on Houston gathered around the Pontiac. "Don't you dare talk to Mr. Tepper that way," an elderly woman shouted at the fat man. She shook her walking stick at him. Somebody else kicked a front fender. A crowd had now gathered, and a couple of people in the crowd started rocking the fat man's car.

". . . then I moved to Kansas, because they don't have a lottery there," the woman who sat in Tepper's Chevy was saying.

"That's what this psychologist I was seeing told my husband we should do, even though I told him I thought what I should do is just keep playing the lottery, because that's the only thing that really gives me pure pleasure. Not that he'd care. He struck me as the sort of person who didn't get any pure pleasure out of anything. Anyway, he told us to move to Kansas, but I guess he didn't know that Missouri has a lottery, and Missouri was real close to where we lived in Kansas, so I'd just go over and play the Missouri lottery. I was in heaven. I love the Missouri lottery . . ."

The fat man was revving his engine, as if he was going to drive into the people standing in front of his car, but nobody moved. Several more people had joined in the rocking. Somebody shouted, "Turn the bastard upside down!" Somebody shouted, "Call the cops!" The elderly woman, who was now banging on the Pontiac's windshield with her walking stick, still shouted, "Don't you dare talk to Mr. Tepper that way!"

The fat man was shouting, "Goddamned spics! I'm going to run you down, you goddamn spics!" His face was a bright red.

Shoppers from Orchard Street, around the corner, gathered to watch the argument. A number of them were still in contentious moods from arguing prices or elbowing each other aside to snatch discount designer dresses off the rack, and most of those who began as onlookers remained to become participants. They argued with each other about Tepper's right to tie up a spot on Sunday on the Lower East Side. Some of them took the fat man's side, so there were half a dozen arguments going on at once between them and Tepper's supporters. "It's a free country," one man kept shouting. "You wouldn't know it sometimes, but it's a free country!" In Tepper's car, the woman in the front seat was saying, "I'd drive into St. Joseph, Missouri, every day. It wasn't far. How I loved St. Joseph, Missouri. It's an older city for that part of the country, the place where the Pony Express . . ." The police arrived almost simultaneously with a camera crew from Channel Five.

16.   *Meeting*

"CAN I GET UP NOW?" MIKE SHANAHAN ASKED AFTER HE had been sitting for almost a full minute in the Body Orifice Security Scanner in the mayor's outer office. "I think I'm already late for the meeting." Even before he'd had to stop at the iris scanner and the BOSS, Shanahan had been held up at the security gate by Eddie, his childhood friend, who, explaining that he'd thought of practically nothing else but Grandma Houlihan's molasses cookies since their last meeting, wouldn't release the turnstile until Mike recited everything he remembered about the recipe.

"Not yet," Teresa said, drawing closer to the machine. "Is that a buzz I'm hearing? Would you say that sound is a soft buzz or just sort of a loud tingle? How would you describe that sound?"

"What sound? I don't hear any sound."

She walked around the machine, cocking her head to catch the sound that Shanahan couldn't hear. "With Commissioner DeSilva this morning, we thought it was just a tingle we were hearing," she said. "And tingles don't count. But it turned out to be an actual buzz. It was set off by his hearing aid. I let him keep it in, of course." Then she studied a manual for a while. Then she said, "You're not, for some reason, holding a tiny dagger in your mouth, are you, Mike?"

"A tiny dagger!" Shanahan said. "You think I've swallowed a miniature Sikh for some reason and he left his tiny dagger in my mouth on the way down? You think I've got designs on trimming the mayor's toenails or something?"

Teresa didn't answer. She simply studied the machine's dials, occasionally referring back to the owner's manual. For a while, it was silent in the mayor's outer office.

Then, suddenly, Shanahan reached inside his mouth and pulled out a wire object that he held in his open palm. "My retainer," he said, in something close to a mumble.

"Your retainer?" Teresa said. "What are you doing with a retainer?"

"The dentist said my lower teeth are getting out of alignment. That happens to be quite common for people of my age. The retainer is just temporary."

"Did you have the retainer when we . . . you know . . ."

"Teresa," Shanahan said, "does it occur to you that we may be approaching the area that some might consider invasion of privacy?"

Teresa, lost in her thoughts, said, "I don't know how I would have felt about you having a retainer. It definitely would have lent a certain high-school quality to the situation. But whether that would have made it more exciting or less exciting, I just don't know. I'm guessing maybe less exciting. . . ."

"Teresa, can I go in now?" Shanahan said. "I promise I won't attack the mayor with my retainer."

"Oh, sure. Go ahead," she said.

The meeting had already begun. Mayor Ducavelli was behind his desk. He showed evidence of having spent some time in the sun when he was in Phoenix for the mayors' conference; his face, which had once been described by a magazine writer as precisely the color of Elmer's glue, looked almost ruddy. He did not look happy. Several of his aides were sitting on chairs and couches arrayed in front of the desk. The gathering had the look of a seminar in the office of someone known to be the toughest marker in the entire university.

Victor Hessbaugh, the city attorney, was speaking. As the city's chief legal officer, Hessbaugh was often the person who had to follow up the mayor's confrontations with legal action—coming up with some interpretation of the regulations governing the city council, for instance, that would permit the mayor to inform a councilwoman who had been critical of his programs that what had been her office had been commandeered for use as a medical supply depot under the terms of the Civil Defense Act of 1952. Hessbaugh was always up to the task. Even in the more bizarre confrontations, Hessbaugh did the mayor's bidding with alacrity, always discovering some way in which Ducavelli was legally justified in doing whatever he wanted to do. Ray Fannon had written that the city attorney "could find legal justification for armed robbery, assuming, of course that Frank Ducavelli happened to be the armed robber." Once the precedent had been found, Hessbaugh would explain it in great detail to anyone who'd listen; he always seemed sincerely convinced by his own loopholes. Given his loyalty, Victor Hessbaugh was known among the City Hall press corps as Victor Yesboss.

". . . the police estimate of the crowd was approximately a hundred and fifty people at the height of the incident," Hessbaugh was saying, occasionally glancing down at the report in his hand. "There were no serious injuries. As you have undoubtedly surmised, that reference in one of the tabloids to someone being hit in the eye with a pickled herring has no basis in fact whatsoever. Pure fantasy. No herrings were thrown. The man who was shown on Channel Five saying, 'Ya jerky bastard, ya,' to the police sergeant had to be restrained at one point, but he was not arrested. Although he'd left his car when the altercation started, and it was ticketed for double parking. None of the people in the crowd around the car were arrested. No charges were brought against Mr. Tepper, who is, as you have probably read, a mailing list broker who not only has no police record but may have never even gotten a parking ticket, which would be remarkable considering how much time he apparently spends parking. The Parking Violations Bureau is checking on that now."

"This happened more than a week ago," Ducavelli said. "The day I left for the mayors' conference. They can't run a check of violations in a week?" The mayor looked at Mark Simpkins, the parking commissioner.

"We've got it on expedited search," Simpkins said.

The mayor's response to that was to roll his eyes. The Parking Violations Bureau was notorious for being the most maddening bureaucracy in the city. Everyone in the room had his favorite PVB story. Shanahan's was of the hospital office worker named Luis Hernandez, who, some years before, had his salary attached for $4,152 by the bureau for back tickets despite the fact that he couldn't drive and had never owned a car. Shanahan could still remember some of the responses newspaper columnists had imagined PVB bureaucrats having to Hernandez's protestations that he'd been dunned in error ("No car! You think we haven't heard that one before? You think you're dealing with a bunch of farmers here, Luis?").

After a short pause, Hessbaugh continued. "Tepper was seeing a series of people in his car," he said. "But the investigating officer noted in his report that even after the altercation had been halted and three people put in the wagon, Mr. Tepper still had seven minutes left on his meter."

"It's legal now to carry on a business in your car?" the mayor almost shouted. "No license is required? Are you telling me that a shoemaker could just put some tools in the backseat and set up shop? What about the honest tradesmen who have to pay rent on their premises and city sales tax on their transactions? What about them?"

"Well, that's a murky area," Hessbaugh said. "You may remember the knife sharpeners who used to go around in little trucks, conducting their business on the street? We've checked to see what kind of licensing they required, but it's doubtful that such licensing would apply to this case anyway, since there's no evidence that Mr. Tepper was charging any of the people who came in to chat with him, so it would be hard to prove that he was running a business. And he was, of course, in a legal spot."

"Legal!" Ducavelli almost shouted. "It's a way to mock the law is what it is. When you strip away all the legalisms, the man's an anarchist. That's what he is—an anarchist. What he's doing is just the sort of thing that could trigger complete chaos. This city would be in the hands of the forces of disorder."

The mayor paused and looked intently at those gathered in front of him. A couple of people shifted nervously in their chairs. Nobody said anything. Then Hessbaugh said, "Apparently, Mr. Tepper uses certain spots on certain days of the week, and since those were mentioned in the press, more people have been waiting to talk to him at those spots, although so far, no other disturbances have—"

The mayor stopped him with a finger wag. It was a gesture, as it happened, not far from the gesture that Tepper sometimes used to stop questions about whether he was going out—although when accomplished in the mayor's peculiarly jerky way of moving, the wag seemed to begin at the shoulder and involve the entire arm. There was more silence. After a few moments, the mayor said, "Any ideas? Am I to assume that nobody has any ideas about how to stop this?"

There was a longer silence. Finally, Mark Simpkins, the parking commissioner, said, rather tentatively, "Well, Mr. Mayor, we could remove the meters from that block in front of Russ & Daughters and make it No Parking Anytime."

The mayor stared at Simpkins. Simpkins smiled weakly. The mayor continued to stare. His lips were pursed and he was nodding slightly. Everyone in the room had seen that nod before. It wasn't a nod of agreement. It was a nod of confirmation—the mayor having confirmed once again that he truly was surrounded by idiots, that he could count on nobody but himself in the fight against the forces of disorder. It was a nod that was often followed by an explosion. "Or even," Simpkins quickly added in a voice that was beginning to sound desperate, "No Standing Anytime. That would, of course, include Sundays."

The mayor didn't say anything. There was silence in the room. Then the mayor began speaking, in a surprisingly soft voice, to Mark Simpkins. "So let me get this plan straight," he said. The others in the room leaned forward to hear. "We're going to get rid of the parking meters on the block of Houston

Street in front of Russ & Daughters. Put in No Standing Anytime. Then when he moves next Sunday to the next block, the Katz's Delicatessen block, we remove the parking meters from that block."

Simpkins was nodding and shrugging tentatively, although it was apparent that what he was hearing from the mayor didn't sound exactly right to him. The mayor was still speaking softly: "Then he moves to the next block. We take away the meters. Then the next block. Sooner or later, this rabble-rouser has forced us to remove all parking meters in the city. Nobody who wants to stop for ten minutes to buy a dozen bagels can do it. We have warehouses full of parking meters. The revenue brought in by the parking meters is gone. Is that the plan? I'm just trying to make sure I understand the plan."

"Well," Simpkins said. "Sort of, only—"

"GET OUT OF THIS OFFICE!" Ducavelli shouted at the top of his lungs. "THAT IS THE MOST IMBECILIC IDEA I'VE EVER HEARD! GET OUT OF HERE!"

Simpkins scurried out of the office. Mayor Ducavelli sat back in his chair, took some deep breaths, and looked around the room. His glance fell on Mike Shanahan. "What do you have on this, Mike?" he said, in a more or less civil tone.

"Well, we did the quickie you asked for when you called from Phoenix," Shanahan said. "Phone survey. A hundred residents, chosen at random. This was four or five days after the hoo-ha in front of Russ & Daughters. It had been on the local news two nights running—although one of those was Sunday night, which is less watched than the weekday newscasts—and in one round of papers, with the *News, Post,* and *Newsday* all carrying it prominently and the *Times* running it on the front page of the Metro section. It was pretty much out of the papers by Tuesday. That's not a sustained period of coverage, really, but, despite that, only eight percent of the respondents said they never heard of Murray Tepper or didn't know enough about what happened to comment. That's remarkable, really. It's axiomatic in the business that if you took a survey the day after the Second Coming at least ten percent would say that they never heard of it or didn't know enough to respond. We asked a spectrum question about what the respondent thinks about Tepper—admires a lot, admires somewhat, doesn't admire at all, et cetera, et cetera—and a few questions designed to ascertain whether the public basically sees him as someone gumming up the works in the city or someone who's standing up for his rights. Then a couple of questions about how this has affected the public perception of you, Mayor."

"And?" Ducavelli said. It was apparent to everyone that the mayor wanted a report on the last series of questions first.

"Well, I know you don't like looking back, Mayor, but in all candor I have to say that when you were asked to comment on this while you were at the conference, it might have been better to have chosen some phrase other than 'a leech on the body politic.' I mean better for your numbers. Generally, people admire Tepper. They think he might be a little eccentric, but just about everyone in this town is a little eccentric. They tend to think that he's got a right to sit in his car if he's in a legal spot and why he's doing it is his own business. Frankly, I was surprised at how few people are irritated at him for taking up a parking spot he doesn't need. I guess they think maybe he does need it, for some reason."

"I'm not guided by what would be better for my numbers," Mayor Ducavelli said.

Shanahan nodded. That was more or less true. Although Frank Ducavelli always did want to know the effect of an issue on his numbers, he often seemed to disregard that information. Some of what seemed like his most intemperate acts did indeed help his numbers—attacking the Ukrainians and the other diplomats at the United Nations over their refusal to pay parking tickets, for instance. He was obviously pleased when railing against the Ukrainians built the public impression of him as a straight shooter who wasn't afraid of any adversary, even an adversary that had a large stockpile of nuclear weapons. But Mike Shanahan had come to believe that Frank Ducavelli might have attacked the Ukrainians even if such an attack were devastating to his numbers. Telling everyone to stand on the sidewalk while hailing a cab obviously wasn't good for his numbers. Putting a homeless shelter in Councilman Norm Plotkin's neighborhood—something Shanahan knew the mayor was perfectly capable of doing—would not be good for his numbers. When the mayor got worked up, he could lose track of how someone who had to run for office ought to behave.

The mayor was silent for a while, and finally his chief of staff let everyone know that the meeting was over.

As Mike Shanahan walked by Teresa's desk, she said, "So how come, then, it didn't buzz the other day?"

"What didn't buzz?"

"The machine. When you sat in it. It didn't go off. Why?"

"Well, unless your machine was on the blink, I guess I wasn't wearing my retainer."

Teresa nodded. "That's what I figured," she said. "You must have had a date."

17. *Hero*

THE HOSTESS SMILED AT MURRAY TEPPER AS SHE LED
him toward the table where Jack was seated. "Medium well man
is here before you," she said.

Tepper smiled and nodded. He had the feeling that two or
three people might have recognized him as he walked through
the restaurant, but then he thought he had probably just imagined that. Most of the customers certainly didn't give him a
glance. Some of them were deep in conversation. At one table
where four people were waiting for their food, three were on cell
phones and the other looked around at photographs of Japan on
the restaurant's walls, like someone who can't find anybody to
talk to at a cocktail party and feigns interest in the books on the
shelves.

He was just sitting down across from Jack when a man who'd
been at a nearby table came over. The man looked to be in his
late thirties or early forties—neatly dressed in a suit and tie. "I'm
terribly sorry to bother you, Mr. Tepper," the man said. "I've
never done anything like this before, but I recognized you from
your picture in the newspaper. I wonder if I could get your autograph for my son, who's eleven. His name is Kevin. He'd seen

the television coverage of the altercation on Houston Street a couple of Sundays ago—the fat man yelling, 'Ya jerky bastard, ya,' and all that—and last night at dinner we talked through the entire incident. He's going to use you as the subject for an essay he has to do for school on courage."

"I have to tell you that there wasn't really any courage involved," Tepper said. "When that fat man started yelling at me, I made sure the doors were all locked and the windows rolled up."

"I mean the courage to do what you think is right," the man said.

"Well, the right and wrong certainly wasn't hard to figure out," Tepper said. "It says right there on the sign that it's One-Hour Metered Parking, Sunday Included, and I was paid up. After it was all over, I still had seven minutes on the meter. No big deal."

The man nodded and put one of the restaurant's place mats in front of Tepper. It was one of those paper place mats for Japanese restaurants which illustrate various types of sushi and sashimi. "His name's Kevin," the man said again. Tepper shrugged and signed the place mat just above the picture of an eel-and-cucumber hand roll.

The man started to turn from the table, but then, after some throat clearing and a couple of false starts, he said, "Mr. Tepper, I've got a little problem at home. Not with Kevin. He's great. A great kid. Soccer team. Does real well in his studies. No, it's his mother—my wife. And she's a fine person, Mr. Tepper. Don't get me wrong. A fine person. That's not the problem. . . ." He looked at Jack and then back at Murray Tepper. "I don't mean to disturb you at lunch," he said.

"Oh, don't mind me," Jack said. "I wouldn't want to interfere with someone seeking professional help."

"I was just wondering if you're still parking on the street now and then—I mean since the incident on Houston Street."

"Oh, yes," Tepper said. "When I can find a legal spot, of course. I only park in legal spots."

The man nodded. "Of course, of course," he said. "I wonder if you're going to be parked anywhere in the early evenings this week. Sunday morning's not really possible for me. I live in the suburbs."

"I was thinking of trying to find a spot on East Seventy-eighth this evening," Tepper said. "Between Lexington and Park."

"Would that really be convenient?" the man asked.

"Oh, yes," Tepper said. "Between Lexington and Park is very convenient, as long as you're not looking for a spot that's going to be good for tomorrow. It's No Parking Eleven A.M. to Two P.M. there. Mondays and Thursdays one side of the street, Tuesdays and Fridays the other. Where the parking gets hard is farther east. Around First Avenue, say, that's murder. Farther up—in the eighties, say, around First Avenue, East End Avenue—it's even worse. Terrible. But between Lexington and Park is very convenient. Very convenient."

"Well maybe I'll see you then," the man said, moving away toward his own table. "And thanks for the autograph."

A waitress approached the table and poured them each a cup of tea. She stood with her order pad at the ready, but she seemed to be suppressing a giggle. She kept her eyes away from Jack.

"Two regular sushis and two Kirin beers," Tepper said.

"Sort of on the rare side," Jack added, causing the waitress's giggle to burst out.

"I don't believe I've ever been with anybody who was asked for an autograph," Jack said. "Unless you count Pete Reiser, of course, and I'm not sure you'd say that I was exactly 'with' Pete Reiser, since I was one of the people asking for his autograph. It does occur to me that the last time we were at this establishment I was suggesting that maybe you might want to consult a shrink and now people are coming up to you and talking about consulting a shrink and the shrink is you."

Tepper nodded, and poured himself some tea. "These things happen," he said.

"Actually, they don't, usually," Jack said. "I think you'll find that it's pretty rare for someone to hint to an old friend, in a kindly and thoughtful way, that the old friend might need a head checkup, maybe just an oil change and lubrication, and the next week there's a survey in the *Post* or the *News* or one of them that sixty-seven percent of the people surveyed say they think it would help their peace of mind or psychological health or whatever to counsel with the old friend in the front seat of his Chevy Malibu, which is legally parked but is otherwise, you'll have to admit, a sort of odd place for a counseling session. I don't think that's the sort of thing that happens regularly. Sixty-seven percent!"

"They tell me that figure's gone up a little," Tepper said. "The survey was taken before Channel Two had the interview with the person who said I'd given him the backbone to ask for a promotion he should have gotten years ago. Funny, I don't remember that person. I watched the interview, and he really doesn't look like anyone I've ever seen before."

"And before the editorial in the *Post*," Jack said.

"Editorial in the *Post*?"

"Of course you haven't seen it," Jack said, "because you still think the *Post* is an afternoon paper, even though everyone else reads it in the morning. I figured that, so I brought it along." He reached into his pocket and unfolded the front page of the *Post*, which had been torn from the rest of the paper. Most of the front page was taken up by a picture of Tepper in his car. Tepper recognized it as one of the shots the photographer from the East Village *Rag* must have taken at the time of the original story by Jeffrey Green. The editorial, set into the picture, was headlined SIMPLE GOOD SENSE FROM AN OLD-FASHIONED GUY. Jack read it out loud:

> In an era when we're constantly being told how complicated everything is, the city has taken to its heart Murray Tepper, a man who somehow finds life simple. Mr. Tepper sits in his car in a legal parking spot simply because it is his right to do so. When he is asked what he's doing there, his answer tends to be simple: "I'm reading the paper." When strangers join Mr. Tepper in the front seat, his advice to them is simple and straightforward. All of them come away feeling better about their lives. Maybe we can all learn something from Murray Tepper. Maybe everything isn't complicated after all.

"Oh, it's complicated all right," Tepper said.

"Are you going to tell me about the complications of some places saying No Parking Eight A.M. to Eleven A.M. and other places saying No Parking Eleven A.M. to Two P.M.?" Jack said.

"Well, that, too," Tepper said. "But I mean all of this publicity. It's brought some complications. A reporter tried to interview Linda when she came out of the apartment to take my grandson to his play group. Richard, of course, is not happy about that.

And it seems to be building. You can't turn on the television without seeing Barney Mittgin, talking about my wisdom and insight; he makes me sound like one of those Indian gurus who always have fifteen Rolls-Royces and a couple of ladies from Shaker Heights to wash their feet. We're getting a mountain of mail at the office every day, and a huge number of e-mails. Almost all in support. Actually, I've got Arnie Sarnow working on what kind of list that could turn out to be. But, all in all, that amount of activity makes it hard for everybody to concentrate on selling the tchotchkes through the mail. Also, I got a call from Sy Lambert, who's some kind of literary agent."

"Some kind of literary agent!" Jack said. "He's in the papers all the time. He's the biggest agent in town. Also the loudest."

"He said when this is all over I'd be able to write a book about what had happened," Tepper said. "The way he put it was that he's sure I have a book in me."

"It sounds like a medical condition," Jack said. "Like kidney stones. It sounds to me like the question was whether they'd have to operate or you might pass it."

Tepper nodded. "It's all taking up a lot of time at the office," he said.

"But, even so, you're still parking—on East Seventy-eighth Street tonight, for instance," Jack said. He made it sound sort of like a question.

"More like early evening," Tepper said. "PBS has a program on Devon and Cornwall at nine, and I promised Ruth I'd be home in time to watch it with her."

18. *Confrontation*

A LOT OF THE PEDESTRIANS AT SEVENTY-EIGHTH AND Park were people coming home from work. They carried briefcases or backpacks or shopping bags or all three at once. Joggers in skimpy costumes—apparently unaware of the mayor's campaign for more modest clothing—were walking toward Central Park, using the wait at a red light to put one foot high on a lamppost and do stretching exercises. Someone who had just parked in front of the entrance to an apartment building was being accosted by a doorman, who kept pointing to a yellow line painted on the curb. Tepper assumed that the parker was a person of some experience who was quite aware that the traffic department didn't use yellow curb lines to denote no parking areas and that the yellow line in front of the building was simply an attempt by the building's management to frighten off the uninformed. The car in question had barely fit into the space in front of the entrance, leaving virtually no room between cars. Anyone coming out of a taxi would have to walk twenty yards to the corner to reach the sidewalk.

"You leave no room," the doorman said, in a heavy Spanish accent.

"Property is theft!" the parker shouted, as he walked away.

The doorman, looking puzzled, shrugged and went back inside the lobby of the building. At around six-thirty, Tepper rounded the corner at Park and began looking for a spot on Seventy-eighth Street.

In two or three places on the block, there appeared to be small crowds of people—not just a few neighbors who'd stopped to chat while walking their dogs but a couple of dozen people looking out toward the street. As he drew nearer, he saw that each crowd was standing near what appeared to be a parking spot. They were waiting for him.

He thought he saw two television trucks double-parked toward the end of the block, almost at Lexington. He also noticed that the first clot of people awaiting him had made a mistake: what looked like a spot was actually governed by a sign farther down the street that said Diplomatic Plates Only. Tepper never parked in Diplomatic Plates Only spots. He resented Diplomatic Plates Only spots, but he didn't park in them. A bit farther down, on the downtown side of the street, he saw a legal spot. It said, NO PARKING 11AM–2PM TUES & FRI. There was plenty of room for his Chevy. It was a beautiful spot. He pulled in front, backed into the spot, turned off the motor, and reached for the *New York Post* on the seat next to him. No sooner had he opened the paper than he heard a knock on the passenger-side window. It was the man he'd spoken to at lunch. Tepper rolled down the window.

"Hello, Mr. Tepper. Remember me from the restaurant today?" the man said. "My name is Alan Harris. I wonder, if you have a few minutes, you'd mind if I joined you?"

"I've got more than a few minutes," Tepper said. "It's Monday, a little after six-thirty, and this place is legal until Tuesday at eleven."

He leaned over and opened the passenger-side door. As Alan Harris got in and sat down, there was some jostling among the people behind him, and Tepper realized that at least part of the crowd was forming a line that led back from the passenger-side door. People from the other little crowds along Seventy-eighth Street had moved to where he was parked. Some of them had joined the line; most of them were just standing next to the wall of an apartment building, watching.

"I really appreciate this," Harris said. "I got here early, but there was soon a crowd. And then whenever a parking spot would open that you might take, we all moved. But there wasn't really any running or pushing. We all just moved the line over to the next spot, and I was still first."

Tepper nodded. "I've always liked an orderly line," he said.

"It's about my wife, Jessica," Harris said, without further introduction. "A very fine person, as I told you at lunch. She writes short stories. She was in that graduate fiction program at Columbia, and then what had been a sort of part-time job with an advertising agency got to be full-time, partly because she was so good at it she just kept getting promoted, and the money was tempting, and then Kevin came along, and, with one thing and another, she's just got back to writing in the last couple of years. But she's already had a couple of stories published in small magazines. Apparently, she's quite talented."

"Apparently?" Tepper asked.

"Well, that's the problem," Harris said. "You see, the sort of thing she writes is not easy for me to judge. She writes what they sometimes call magic realism. It's a style of fiction writing, mainly in Latin America. Most of the writers are from places like Argentina and Chile. My wife happens to be the rare Connecticut magic realist. So the magic stuff—some of the stuff that you're not sure whether it's a dream, and there are a lot of serpents and things—happens at places like shopping malls or school plays. But it's the same sort of writing. In her stories, there are things that happen that you never can tell for sure are supposed to have really happened. I mean, this woman is supposed to be having a baby but it's a goat. Or maybe it's a baby that looks like a goat. Or maybe it was a dream. Or maybe the whole story is supposed to be a dream and the woman herself is not real. You know what I mean?"

Tepper nodded. As it happened, he told Harris, he had a certain familiarity with the subject. He had once had a client who was convinced that a strong connection could be made between magic realism and magic, meaning that people who had sent away for books by writers like Jorge Luis Borges and Gabriel García Marquez would be a good market for a magic set that included six surefire tricks (with instructions), a top hat, and a wand. Tepper was able to summarize his view of that notion in one old-fashioned New York word—cockamamie—but to satisfy the client he did a small test mailing. The test indicated that readers of magic realism had slightly less than the normal interest in magic tricks.

Harris seemed encouraged to know that Tepper understood what he was talking about. "The problem is that I just don't get this kind of thing. I'm a civil engineer, Mr. Tepper. I mean, I'm more or less in the sales end now, but my training was as an engineer. To me a thing is pretty much what it is. A baby is a baby. A goat is a goat."

"So you can't really comment very well on your wife's stories?"

"Right. Exactly. It's understandable for someone who started writing stories sort of late—or came back to it sort of late, really—to be worried about being taken for a housewife who's dabbling. And I can see in my wife's face when we talk about one of her stories that she thinks I'm just sort of patting her on the head and saying, 'That's nice, dear.' I know it's very painful for her."

"My wife does watercolors," Tepper said. "She's also quite talented, they say. I'm not a real connoisseur of art. I did do an art campaign once. The same genius who thought there was a connection between magic realism and magic tricks was convinced that you could sell reproductions of great art through the mail by using the subjects of the paintings rather than the style. At first it didn't seem too crazy—say, using subscription lists of ballet magazines to sell Degas reproductions. Sooner or later, though, he got to believing that to sell that famous picnic scene Manet painted all we needed to do was get hold of a list of people who had sent away for fancy picnic baskets. That sort of thing. We would have done just as well with lists of people who had sent away for books by Jorge Luis Borges. Nothing!"

Harris nodded, politely waiting for Tepper to enlighten him on what that had to do with the problem of being married to a Connecticut magic realist. The line outside the car was getting longer. The people weren't shouting to hurry or knocking on the window—for New Yorkers, they were being remarkably polite—but they did seem to be edging closer to the window, as if taking up some of the slack space between them and the car would get them in faster.

"Anyway," Tepper finally said. "I don't know a lot about composition and all that. And a lot of watercolors of landscapes or fishing wharfs look pretty much the same to me—all very nice, of course, but pretty much the same. But my wife gets a blue in her paintings that I truly love. I genuinely love that blue. It's a terrific blue."

Tepper stopped talking and just sat there nodding his head, as if thinking about how much he liked his wife's blue. Harris didn't say anything for a while.

Then he said, "Do you mean I should look for something in my wife's work that I can truly get excited about?"

Tepper looked impressed. "That might be an idea," he said.

"You know," Harris said. "She is really great at describing serpents. I can't say I always know why the serpents are coming out of people's noses, and, well, other places, but when she starts talking about that serpent you can just see it right there in front of your eyes. You get sort of edgy about having the thing wrap itself around you. Actually, it's terrifying. I'm not sure I've ever told her how really blown away I am by her serpents."

"I like seeing a nice serpent now and then," Tepper said. "When I take my grandson to the zoo, the snake and lizard house is our third favorite place, after the chimpanzees and the tigers. By the way, people who have shown an interest in snakes and other reptiles have no more than the normal interest in buying those really tough leather boots that are supposed to protect you from snakebites. We found that out the hard way."

Harris glanced out the window at the line. "Listen, Mr. Tepper," he said, "I really can't thank you enough for—"

He was interrupted by a loud knocking on the driver's-side window. Both Tepper and Harris looked over. A large police sergeant was standing in the street, signaling for the window to be rolled down. When Tepper had lowered it halfway, the policeman said, in a tone that seemed overly polite for a New York police-man, "Excuse me, sir. I'm afraid I have to issue you a summons."

"There must be some mistake, Sergeant," Tepper said. "This spot is legal until tomorrow morning at eleven A.M. Possibly you have it mixed up with the spot down the street that says Diplo-matic Plates Only. I never park in Diplomatic Plates Only spots."

"It's not exactly a parking ticket, sir," the sergeant said, con-sulting a card he held in his hand. "It's for being in contraven-tion of the city ordinance against unlicensed demonstrations or exhibitions that could, because of crowds or other effects, be a danger to the public or the public peace."

"I'm not familiar with that ordinance," Tepper said.

Another voice, from behind the police sergeant, said, "It has been on the books since 1911, it is a Class C misdemeanor, an-swerable in person in criminal court, and it is roughly compar-able to the concept in civil law of an 'attractive nuisance.'" The person who had spoken stepped in front of the policeman and introduced himself: "I am Victor Hessbaugh, the city attorney of New York."

Just behind Hessbaugh, a large man who was wearing a *Prairie Home Companion* T-shirt said, "Hey, there's a line here, buddy."

As Hessbaugh went into more detail about the summons—how soon it had to be answered, the acceptable methods of pay-ing the fine, the offices in Manhattan and other boroughs where the fine could be paid, the court where a not guilty plea could be entered—the man in the T-shirt repeated, "There's a line here!"

For the first time, Tepper saw television cameras. Two cam-eramen had apparently moved to the front of the crowd when the sergeant appeared. One of them got shoved backwards as the crowd suddenly shifted. The man in the T-shirt had elbowed

Hessbaugh aside and was immediately grabbed by the sergeant who had given Tepper the summons.

"Hey, let him go!" someone in the crowd shouted. "He was next!"

The crowd surged forward, and the frightened face of Victor Hessbaugh suddenly appeared, flattened, against Tepper's window. The police sergeant was shouting now, and pulling at the man in the T-shirt, who kept saying, "I've been here since five-thirty, goddamn it!" For a couple of minutes, it appeared that Victor Hessbaugh's face was going to be flattened against the Chevy's window for the foreseeable future, but then a couple of police vans screeched to a halt next to Tepper's car, and a squad of policemen carrying billy clubs climbed out. Within a few minutes, the crowd was moved away from the car.

"All right, it's all over here," a policeman with captain's bars on his shoulder kept saying. "Let's move it out. Nothing left to see. Nothing left to see. Let's go on home now, folks."

Harris and the others drifted off. Tepper, finding himself alone again, picked up the *Post*. Then he noticed another figure standing on the sidewalk—a man carrying a couple of shopping bags that bore the logo of the local supermarket. It was Ray Fannon, the columnist. In one bag, Fannon had mostly diet drinks and club soda. In the other bag he had the potato chips and corn nuts and peanuts he put out on the table for the poker game—what the regulars called Fannon's gourmet treats. Fannon was on his way home. His apartment was just down the street, and it was poker night.

19. *Who's Crazy Now?*

BY THE TIME THE REGULARS ARRIVED FOR FANNON'S poker game, the only sign that there had been a disturbance on Seventy-eighth Street was the presence of one television reporter, a late arrival, who, standing in the Diplomatic Plates Only space, was doing a wrap-up that included an interview with an apartment house super who'd seen everything. ("The man was legally parked. No question in my mind.") Following the longtime custom at Fannon's game, most of the discussion of what had happened was put off until after the final hand—one hand of a game called Discards Wild, dealt by Bart Adams, who also seemed to be the only person at the table to grasp the rules.

"So, was Yesboss really smashed up against the car when you got there?" Chuck Gold asked Fannon, the moment the game was over. Adams was raking in the chips from the final pot. Most of the other players had folded, some of them because of weak cards and some of them because of a total lack of understanding of what constituted weak cards.

"I'm afraid Yesboss could have lost some bridgework for the cause," Fannon said. "The odd thing is that even with his face in a shape that could be fairly described, I think, as one-dimensional, he still seemed to be talking. I suppose he was continuing to explain in great detail why this was perfectly legal, the way he explained in great detail why everything was perfectly legal that time when City Hall managed to evict the Head Start program from P.S. 4's building after the director said 'Hail, Caesar' when he was introduced to the mayor. I can't be certain of that, though. He couldn't move his lips much, so it was hard to understand exactly what he was saying. It was like listening to a very bad ventriloquist."

"I can't believe Il Duce is doing this," Chuck Gold said. "It's obvious that there's tremendous sympathy in the city for this guy Tepper."

"It's really screwy," Steve Lopez said. "People love Tepper for standing up and doing what he wants to do. They seem to see him as a big rebel—someone engaged in principled civil disobedience or something like that. But the whole point is that he's in a legal spot. He's not disobedient at all. When it's all over, he's got seven minutes left on the goddamn meter."

"But what can Ducavelli get out of this?" Brian Higgins said. "Going against Tepper is bound to be bad for his numbers—right, Mike? I mean, is there any way this could be good for his numbers?"

"Well, I suppose if Yesboss pokes around enough there's an outside chance of finding that Tepper has some connection to the Ukrainian delegation to the United Nations," Shanahan said.

"I'm afraid not," Steve Lopez said. "I heard that both sides of his family were originally from Lithuania. That delegation happens to have very few unpaid tickets. It may be that they have a paucity of drivable cars."

"Well, there goes our silver lining," Shanahan said. "Failing that, there's no way it could be good for his numbers, and I, as the chief executive officer of the political polling firm that he has had the wisdom to hire, told him that. Our quickie the other night showed that the citizens of every age and race and income level admire Murray Tepper, even if he's taking up a spot they might be able to use—an expression of mass unselfishness that is, as far as I know, unprecedented in this city."

"And Carmody *is* running," Bart Adams said, looking up from where he was piling his Discards Wild winnings in even stacks to turn in. "My quickie showed the same results, and Carmody's sure to jump all over this. It's just his sort of thing: Il Duce bullying a little guy who just wants to be left alone to read the afternoon paper and talk to the folks. I'd bet this pot that Maxie Allen's already at work on the music for some ditty like 'When They Hauled Me Away I Had Time on the Meter and You.'"

"So why is Ducavelli doing this?" Higgins said.

"Why does a compulsive person spend a lot of time organizing his bolts and screws and nuts and nails by size when he knows perfectly well there are better ways to spend his time?" Adams said. "Because he can't help himself. He's gotten himself so worked up about the forces of disorder that he's even afraid of somebody who's overwhelmingly orderly."

"So it gets back to what I've been saying all along," Higgins said. "People think Carmody's crazy and Ducavelli's rational, but it's the opposite. Carmody would never do anything that's bad for his numbers."

"Do you realize what you're saying?" Gold said. "What you're saying is that a politician who does anything that is not good for his numbers—that is, in other words, not in his political self-interest—can be considered mentally unbalanced."

They all nodded soberly. "I'll go for that," Fannon said.

20. *Aftermath*

THREE DAYS LATER, AT THE OFFICES OF WORLDWIDE lists, Murray Tepper pushed aside a large pile of rate cards he'd been perusing and began to reread Ray Fannon's column in the *Daily News*. "This week, I saw a large crowd gathered around a man who has no interest in drawing attention to himself," the column began.

> Amidst the strivers and climbers and hustlers who are drawn to this city, Murray Tepper is that New Yorker too rarely encountered by a newspaper columnist—a man who simply wants to be left alone. He's polite to reporters, but he doesn't cultivate them. He's patient with those who want to tell him their stories, but he doesn't claim any special wisdom. He's a man who likes to sit in his car—legally parked—and read the news-paper. If he hadn't been reading a rival newspaper when last I saw him, I'd be tempted to call him a model citizen.

"Am I interrupting, Murray?"

Tepper looked up from his desk. Howard Gordon was stand-ing at the door of the office.

"Of course not, Howard, come in," Tepper said. "I was just taking a break from going through some of these old rate cards to see if there's any way we can go further with that connection we found between accountants and designer blue jeans. I wish I understood it better. There is no doubt that if you're trying to sell men's designer jeans there is no better list than a list of accountants. We stumbled into that with some discount designer jeans—Arnie found it, really. But what exactly is the connection? The discount had nothing to do with it; they're just as eager to buy full-price designer jeans. And it doesn't seem to have anything to do with their interest in numbers. We've tested mathematicians, for instance, and people who work in banks. Nothing. Then we thought maybe in some way it had some connection with professions that lounge comics like to make jokes about, so we tried it with dentists. Nothing. Well, not nothing—a slight bump over lists of other professions, but not enough of a bump to be commercially significant. So, it remains a mystery."

"My brother-in-law wears designer blue jeans," Gordon said. "Always with a very pronounced crease."

"And? I can't remember—is he an accountant?"

"No, he sells appliances."

Tepper waited for a moment, to see if something followed that. Nothing did. "Well," Tepper finally said, "what can I do for you, Howard?"

"I just dropped by to see how you're holding up, with all this stuff, Murray. Is the summons something to worry about?"

"It doesn't seem very serious," Tepper said. "Maybe a hundred-dollar fine, tops, I'm told—although I'm not sure I completely understand it. This lawyer for the city really did try to explain it. I'll give him that. But with his face pushed up against the window he was hard to make out."

"We could call Stan Lerner," Gordon said. "He's not a criminal lawyer, of course, but maybe he could recommend somebody."

"Actually, I got a call from someone at the Civil Liberties Union," Tepper said. "Jeremy Thornton. He said they would like to represent me, but if they did they would take it to court rather than pay the fine. No fee to me for their services. He said they believe that this ordinance the lawyer with his face in the window was talking about is unconstitutional, at least in the way the city employed it. They think it violates the Constitution's guarantee of the right of free assembly. They'd like to test its constitutionality."

"That makes it sound pretty important—testing its constitutionality. Of course, it would still be a drag for you—testifying, meeting with them, press conferences, all that sort of thing. More reporters."

"Oh, it probably wouldn't be so bad," Tepper said.

"Are there still a lot of letters coming in?"

"Oh, yes. Letters. E-mails. Phone calls. All that has increased a lot in volume since the business on Seventy-eighth Street Monday night. I've got Arnie testing out the list we're making of the names. You know I hate to leave any list untested. Actually, I told him to go ahead and get a Taunton test done. You never know."

Gordon nodded, and said, "Sure. Fine. I saw Barney Mittgin on one of the news shows, by the way. He seemed in good spirits."

"Barney's pretty happy," Tepper said. "Every time he gets interviewed for television or one of the papers he tells the story about how I thought of testing the computer-repair magazine list for his pillow and how brilliant that was. Actually, the test drew a one-point-one response, which wasn't enough to justify using the list, but I gave up trying to tell Barney that after the eighth or ninth time. Anyway, he's mentioned the map-pillow in that story so much that some people apparently started to look for it in the few catalogs he got it in, and he's finally moving some of them. Also, his cousin in Detroit saw him on television and now thinks he's a big shot, and that's worth a lot more than pillow sales to Barney. For the first time since we've been in business, I think you could call him a satisfied customer."

"Murray," Gordon said, "where's this all going—this parking? I mean, what's going to happen?"

Tepper looked at his partner. Was he just imagining it, or did Howard look sadder than ever? "Well, I'm not sure, Howard," Tepper said. "Maybe—"

Tepper was interrupted by the buzzer on his desk, and the voice of Hilda, the receptionist. "Murray, you said to remind you at four that you absolutely had to leave for an appointment with a Mr. Lambert."

Tepper thanked her, and stood up. Gordon took a step or two toward the door. "I'm sorry, Howard," Tepper said. "We'll have to talk about that Monday. I've got this appointment."

"Sure, of course," Gordon said, as they neared the door of Worldwide Lists. "This is Sy Lambert, the big agent, if I may ask?"

Tepper nodded. "We arranged to meet at his office, on Fifty-seventh Street," he said.

"Murray, I hope you don't mind my asking—you're not planning to drive there, are you?"

Tepper stopped at the door. "Howard," he said. "Please. It's four o'clock in the afternoon, on a weekday. I'm supposed to go up to the West Side, get my car, and drive it down to Fifty-seventh Street, to a block that's going to be No Parking Nine to Seven at best? Now that would be eccentric. Maybe not a misdemeanor, but certainly eccentric."

Howard Gordon nodded. "Good," he said, as if welcoming the news of a very small victory. "Fine, Murray. We'll talk about it later."

When Tepper emerged from the building, he started to walk toward the subway. He was still a bit ahead of rush hour. Because of the warm weather, the air-conditioning inside the trains had been turned on, but the weather hadn't been warm enough to build up the heat in the stations; there was still a month or so to go before the system had created what Tepper always thought of as the New York version of the Swedish sauna, offering, instead of an abrupt change from a hot tub to freezing snow, an abrupt change from furnace-like stations to freezing trains and back again.

Suddenly, a bike messenger jumped the curb in the space next to a fire hydrant, rode up on the sidewalk, and screeched to a halt in front of Tepper. The messenger appeared to be young, but it was difficult to tell, since part of his costume consisted of a sort of burnoose wrapped partly around his face. The burnoose was black and so were his shirt and trousers. He carried a huge black leather pack on his back. "You're my man, Murray," the messenger said, extending to Tepper a greasy black glove. "Stick to your guns. You just keep on parking, man!"

"Thanks very much," Tepper said, shaking the messenger's hand.

"Let me tell you what that freaky mayor wants to do to bike messengers."

"Well, actually, I have an appointment—"

The messenger began a detailed, surprisingly scholarly account of a proposal Mayor Ducavelli had made for bringing order to bicycle traffic in the streets—a proposal that, as the messenger told the story, would destroy the bike-messenger industry and, for all practical purposes, end communication among businesses in Manhattan. Finally, Tepper was able to break away, but he decided it was too late to take the subway. Spotting an empty taxi moving in his direction, he stepped out in the street and raised his hand to hail it. Just as the taxi stopped, Tepper felt a hand on his arm. He turned, expecting to encounter someone with a specious claim about having been waiting there ahead of him. Instead, he found himself facing a policeman.

"You're breaking the ordinance against hailing a taxi out in the street," the policeman said, drawing out a summons book. "You got any identification?"

As he pulled out his wallet, Tepper could hear shouting from the sidewalk. It was the bike messenger. He was pulling out his cell phone as he talked. "They can't get away with this, Murray," he said. "I'm calling Channel Five News Tips. Stick to your guns, Murray!"

21. *Important People*

SY LAMBERT'S OFFICE WAS IN A SLICK NEW BUILDING
that had several huge trees growing in an otherwise spare lobby,
as if they'd wandered over from Central Park by mistake. The
suite of offices marked SY LAMBERT, AUTHOR'S REPRESENTATIVE
seemed to be mainly dark wood and framed photographs. The
photographs were all portraits, blown up to five or six times the
size of portraits usually found on office walls. Some were of
people Tepper thought of as authors, but most of them were of
assorted celebrities—actors, anchormen, the showier real estate
developers, even one bullfighter. All of the portraits were
inscribed to Sy Lambert, but not with just a line or two of script.
They all had at least a full paragraph. The texts read less like
inscriptions on photographs than like honorary degree citations, or maybe even eulogies. The portrait of a man who owned
a couple of sports teams—a man Tepper had often read about on
the sports pages as notorious for meddling with his managers
and firing people capriciously—began, "To Sy Lambert. Sy Lambert is more than simply the finest author's representative in the
United States—or, really, in the world. He is a person of great
vision, of incredible integrity. In any company, Sy Lambert
would be, to put it mildly . . ." Tepper read on for another few

sentences before the receptionist said, "Mr. Tepper, Mr. Lambert can see you now. Let me take you back."

They walked through a hall lined with the same sorts of huge portraits that were in the reception area. Tepper was ushered into a vast office. Here the inscribed portraits seemed even larger, but they didn't take up all the wall space. There were also paintings, and Tepper, before he thought about it, stopped for a moment to take a closer look at one that seemed familiar, maybe from the scheme to sell reproductions through the mail. It was a picture of a table that looked almost, but not quite, real. The colors were arresting.

"Hockney!" said a booming voice from across the room.

Tepper looked behind him. "Hockney," Sy Lambert repeated, stepping out from behind a huge desk that, if Tepper wasn't mistaken, rested on a small platform. "The picture is by David Hockney. You'll never guess what I paid for it."

Tepper shrugged and shook his head, trying to indicate that he would have no idea of what such a painting would cost.

"Go ahead—guess. You'll never guess. So guess!"

Tepper shook his head again. He didn't know whether Lambert was boasting that he paid a lot for the painting—that he was rich and could afford to pay a lot—or that he had paid very little for it, having been shrewd enough to buy it before David Hockney's prices went up. He also didn't know which of those any figure would signify.

"Klee!" Lambert boomed, pointing to a painting on the opposite wall. "I paid a bloody fortune for that one, but I had to have it. It spoke to me." From that remark, Tepper decided that Lambert had paid an impressively high price rather than an impressively low price for the Hockney.

Lambert stood silently for a few moments in front of the Klee. He was a large man with a large head, large features, and large glasses. He was heavy, but not in the bulging sausage-casing way that Barney Mittgin was heavy. Lambert seemed to be someone who'd added another chest and stomach right on top of his original chest and stomach. He had, in effect, a second front. He was in his shirtsleeves—one of those shirts that was blue except for its collar, which was exceedingly white. He was wearing large gold cuff links. He was also wearing a dark blue tie that swelled out over his second front.

Lambert motioned Tepper to one of the chairs that was gathered around a sort of coffee table at one end of the office, and settled into another of the chairs himself.

"You're going to be famous, Murray," he said. "Which means you're going to be rich. In this country, thanks to people like me, 'rich' and 'famous' are almost the same word."

Tepper smiled and shrugged. "Well, I'm not sure famous," he said.

"Oh, no—famous!" Lambert said. "Now you're known. Soon you'll be famous. You know why? Because the mayor's going to make you famous. Do you know the mayor?"

"Not personally," Tepper said.

"I know the mayor," Lambert said. "Naturally. I know him well. I met him years ago through Luciano Pavarotti. Well, not exactly through Luciano, but because Luciano was in town and I said to the person with him—big Italian magnate, very big—that maybe we should get together sometime for a Knicks game, because I've had season tickets for years and my seats happen to be four rows behind Spike Lee's seats. But that's another story— the whole Knicks business. The point is that the mayor won't be able to stop himself from trying to crush you, because you offend his sense of order. He can't help himself. I saw him after he decided this crazy business with taxis—that people have to hail taxis from the sidewalk. I said, 'Frankie . . .'—I've always called him Frankie. I said, 'Frankie, I just told the governor this morning at breakfast'—I was having breakfast with the governor at the Regency—'that you're making a big mistake.' He said, 'Sy, a rule is a rule.' So you're going to be famous, Murray. That means you're going to have a big book. You're going to be a big author. No, not big—huge. There's a movie, of course. That's one of the reasons we want to do the book—so the movie has to be based on the rights to that, instead of some pissant little newspaper story or something. I've already got some calls in about the movie. But we start with your book."

"I've never really written anything," Tepper said.

"Who said anything about writing?" Lambert said. "Writers aren't big authors. They don't do the really huge books. Oh, maybe one or two of them—Stephen King, the Harry Potter gal. These are exceptions. Remember the days when writers would live in garrets and dream of writing a great book and becoming famous? They had it backwards, Murray. Most of them were just wasting their time. The point is to become famous and then write the book. Really big books are by-products of fame, Murray. Remember that: Really big books are by-products of fame. Publishers try to make books big by figuring out how to get noticed off the book page, but the biggest books are by people who are off the book page to start with. The big authors are big because they're famous— they're famous politicians or famous CEOs or famous adulterers. The point is, they're famous. That's what you're going to be."

Lambert sat back in his chair, smiling. Then, suddenly, he said, "Jasper Johns!"

Tepper nodded. He knew about Jasper Johns through the art-through-the-mail scheme. "Jasper Johns is famous," he said. "I didn't know he was an author."

"No! No! The painting behind you is by Jasper Johns," Lambert said. "Guess how much I paid for it."

Tepper shrugged. He was hoping Lambert's attention would be deflected before an answer was required, as it had been when he'd asked Tepper to guess how much the Hockney had cost and then had started talking about something else. But Lambert fell silent. Finally, Tepper said, "I wouldn't really . . ."

"No, go ahead—guess," Lambert said.

"I don't know much about . . ."

"Guess!" Lambert said, in a loud voice.

"Well, I'm not actually someone who . . ."

"Guess, goddamn it!" Lambert said. He was actually shouting now, and his face looked dangerously red. "Just guess! Just guess how much I paid for the goddamned picture!"

Fortunately for Tepper, a secretary entered the room. "Mr. Lambert," she said, "you wanted to be informed if the ambassador phoned. He's on line three."

Lambert nodded, and got up to go to his desk. After a few steps, he turned back toward Tepper—it was almost as if he'd suddenly remembered Tepper's presence—and said, in a perfectly calm voice, "I've got to take this one. The ambassador's an old, old friend. We'll get together soon, Murray. Don't forget: you're going to be famous. And rich. But, of course, we know those are the same thing."

22. *Sabbath Gasbags*

THE PANELISTS WERE GATHERED IN COMFORTABLE-looking swivel chairs around a small table. A large photograph of the Capitol was behind them as a backdrop. They were just putting the finishing touches on a discussion of whether a senator from the Midwest—a strong environmentalist—had ended his political career by acknowledging that the rumors about his romantic fling with a natural-gas lobbyist were true. There were, in addition to the moderator, four panelists—four out of the battalion of Washington journalists and quasi journalists who appeared on television every Sunday morning to pontificate on the events of the previous week. Tepper had once heard such people described as the Sabbath Gasbags, and, as he and Ruth watched the program in the room that the Teppers sometimes called the den and sometimes the TV room, he thought of the figures on the screen as, almost literally, gasbags. He could imagine them floating just above their chairs, occasionally emitting little squeaks as a bit of gas escaped.

Murray and Ruth Tepper were at opposite ends of a couch, with the Sunday *New York Times* in between them. Tepper had already read the Sunday edition of the *News*, in which Ray Fannon had written, apropos of Tepper's taxi-hailing summons, "Although City Hall insists that Mr. Tepper was not singled out by a police department that now seems to be in charge of protecting the citizenry from finding taxicabs, suspicions to the contrary were reinforced when the mayor, retreating to the sarcasm he often uses like a blunderbuss, pointed to the summons as an indication that 'Mr. Tepper might not be the model citizen the press would have us all believe.' City Hall's reassurances were also not helped, of course, by the fact that Mayor Ducavelli has become to vindictiveness what the early New York Mets were to infield errors."

Occasionally, one of the Teppers reached over and picked up a section of the paper, the way people having drinks will sometimes reach over into the mixed nuts. Murray Tepper had the Week in Review on his lap, but, unlike his wife, he was concentrating on the screen rather than on the newspaper. The gasbag who was speaking said, "He's got three and a half years before he has to face the voters, who have twice in the past given him solid victories, even, in his last campaign, after some other old rumors became an issue. There's every reason to believe that by the time the next election comes around the voters in his state will have put all of this into perspective."

"Ralph?" the moderator said, turning to a neatly dressed man with the appearance of a regional auditor who hadn't been outside for a long time.

"Well, I certainly hope they will not 'put it in perspective,'" Ralph said. "Entirely too much has been 'put in perspective' in this country. The American people are sick to death of being asked to put things into perspective. They want public servants who are not morally suspect. They expect public figures to maintain high moral standards, and not to wallow in the filth of extramarital affairs. They do not think it's too much to ask of a senator that he keep the oath he made to be faithful to his wife. For what this man has done, there is no 'perspective.'"

Tepper sighed. He wondered how people like Ralph Simmental always knew exactly what the American people thought. Also, he remembered reading that Simmental himself had once strayed so seriously from his wedding vows that his wife, waiting until he had left for the office one morning, piled all of his expensive television roundtable suits in the front yard and set them on fire—an event that made the newspapers because a neighbor, fearing the blaze was about to get out of hand, called the fire department.

Ruth, apparently having heard the sigh, said, "Shall we turn that off? I'm not so sure it's good for you to watch these people on Sunday. Either you sigh or you mutter or you groan. I think it's bad for your digestion, Murray."

Tepper, without saying anything, flicked his hand in a gesture Ruth always took to mean "leave it" or "never mind" or "later" and people looking for a parking space always took to mean that Tepper was not going out. Ruth shrugged, and went back to the *Times*.

The moderator, turning to look directly into the camera, ended the discussion by summarizing the sense of the panel on whether the senator's career was over or not: "It's too soon to tell." Then he shifted in his seat a bit, and gazed purposefully into another camera. "And, finally, this morning," he said, "we have a story from New York that I suppose you might say could only happen in New York. It concerns a certain Murray Tepper, who may or may not be Everyman, or at least the New York version of Everyman."

Ruth put down the Travel section of the *Times*, where she had been reading about the cheapest airfares to England. "Oh my goodness!" she said, very slowly. Murray Tepper didn't change his expression.

"This is a man who has lived in New York all of his life," the moderator went on. "He has always been a law-abiding citizen, a responsible citizen who has his own business in the direct-mail industry. He has been parking in New York in legal parking spots, and then staying in his car, sometimes to chat with people who seem to value his counsel and advice, sometimes simply to read the newspaper. The mayor—Frank Ducavelli, who, as you know, is such a stickler for order that the local papers refer to him as Il Duce—says Mr. Tepper is causing trouble. Mr. Tepper says there is no trouble as long as he has time on the meter. What are we to make of all this? Ralph?"

"This should serve as a lesson for all our liberal friends who think that the way to fix anything is to pass another law," Ralph Simmental said. "Mr. Tepper is actually obeying the law, and yet it is he who needs fixing."

"What lesson?" said another panelist, a rumpled man who was settled deeply into his swivel chair and had seemed in danger of falling asleep. "What harm is he doing? The man is just sitting there reading the paper. For all we know, he may be reading Ralph's column. I don't understand where the lesson comes in. The lesson is: Leave him alone."

"If he was reading my column, then he'd know that I have advised him to get another hobby," Simmental replied. "There have already been two public disturbances caused by this supposedly law-abiding citizen. You would be within the law to drive at thirty-five miles an hour on the freeway, but if a lot of people did that, the traffic around our cities would be disastrous. The American people are sick to death of people taking advantage of laws and then playing victim. This man is not a victim. He's a provocateur. Simple as that."

"Actually," the only woman on the panel said, "the polls in New York show that the American people are not sick to death of Murray Tepper. They admire him, even though he is often taking up one of their parking spaces."

"Those are not the American people," Simmental said, almost shuddering. "Those are the New York people."

"You know, I always wondered why there were people in their cars who weren't going out," said the only panelist who hadn't yet spoken, a bearded man who worked for a midwestern newspaper. "When I lived in New York I used to get irritated when you thought somebody was about to leave and he just shook his head. It seemed willful. Selfish. But now that I've met Murray Tepper—at least through the press coverage—I feel a lot better about those people. It sort of personalized the whole thing for me. Now I think, okay, you want to sit in your car for a while, sit in your car for a while. Of course this is easier to say for me now, because I no longer live in New York. If he were in Washington, I might want him locked up."

"The fact that it's personalized for you doesn't make it right," Simmental said. "Perhaps you would have felt better about revolutionaries if you got to know Che Guevara and found out how charming he could be. It's simply irrelevant."

"Che Guevara!" Ruth said, slapping the Travel section on the coffee table for emphasis. "He's got his nerve!"

Tepper patted Ruth on the arm, and said, "He doesn't mean anything by it. That's just the way he talks."

"Well, you can compare him to Che Guevara if you want to," the panelist who had once lived in New York said, "but I think to a lot of people—not just New Yorkers but people across the country—Murray Tepper has become a hero."

The moderator said something about continuing to follow the story as it developed. Tepper turned off the television, and got up from the couch.

"So I'll be back in an hour or two," he said. "The kids are coming for lunch, right?"

Ruth nodded. "Are you going out to park?"

"Right," Murray said.

"Murray, is it okay—I mean with the police and all?"

"Oh yes, I think it's okay."

"Are you going down there to Houston Street in front of Russ & Daughters?"

"Right," Tepper said. "Although I don't know if I'll be able to find a spot right in front. It's a little late."

"Listen," Ruth said. "While you're down there, why don't you pick up a pound of herring salad and a whitefish?"

"A nice whitefish?"

"Yes, that would be good—a nice whitefish."

23. *No Spots*

TEPPER TOOK SEVENTH AVENUE INTO BROADWAY, TURNED east on Twenty-third Street and then south again on Second Avenue—a route that would offer him an opportunity to tip his hat as he passed the Second Avenue Deli, a place he treasured because its mushroom and barley soup tasted like the mushroom and barley soups of his childhood. At Houston, he turned left, past Yonah Schimmel's legendary knishery, which had been there as long as he could remember. As he approached the Russ & Daughters block, he could see that the sidewalk, which got crowded on any Sunday morning, was jammed with people. A covey of television news trucks had preceded him. They were lined up in front of Russ & Daughters, presumably awaiting Murray Tepper, but there were so many of them and they were of such size that there was noplace left for him to park.

As Tepper's Chevy rolled slowly past the TV trucks, a couple of men waved him down. "We're from Channel Five, Mr. Tepper," one of them said. "We were hoping you could park here, right in front of the store." He pointed to a spot a few feet away that was occupied by a Ford Taurus.

"But there's someone in that spot," Tepper said.

"She was about to leave," the other man from Channel Five said.

"I was not," came a shout from the car. "I was not about to leave. Don't say that I was about to leave, because it simply isn't true." It sounded like the voice of an elderly woman, and to Tepper there was something familiar about it.

"What kind of business is this?" the Taurus driver went on. "Every hooligan with a sound truck thinks he's the king of the streets. They're making a movie, you're supposed to disappear from your own block. You're a problem for them, being alive in front of your own house. They're shooting some silly news story, some cat up in a tree except there's a lot of gunfire, you're supposed to not exist. Tell Mr. Hooligan I've got forty minutes on the meter, and when that runs out, I'm putting in another four quarters." The speaker stuck her head out of the window of her car, and opened her palm to show the quarters.

For the first time, Tepper got a look at the driver of the Taurus. "Miss Goldhurst?" he said.

"Hello, Murray," Miss Goldhurst said. "I can't say you haven't changed a bit since fifth grade, but you don't look so bad for an old fellow."

"Miss Goldhurst, I'm surprised to see you," Tepper said.

"You mean you're surprised to see me alive. You probably thought all of your teachers were ancient when you were at P.S. 128, and you can't believe that one of them is still breathing. Actually, at least two of them are still breathing. Remember Mr. Hogan, the gym coach? He's older than I am and he's still breathing. He needs a bit of oxygen now and then, but he's still breathing. We live near each other in darkest Queens."

"You come in here from Queens to get lox?"

"I came in to see you, Murray. How many of my old fifth-graders make the newspapers? You're about it. Well, Larry Talbot made the papers, of course. Think of it: one of our own P.S. 128 boys indicted for the single largest tax evasion charge in the history of the United States of America! That was something. But to talk to Larry I would have had to go to Belize or Bahrain or wherever he snuck off to. Good at math, Larry Talbot. Not a lovely boy in many ways, but you have to say that about him—very good at math."

Some of the pedestrians who had been drawn by the television news vans drifted over to stand between Tepper's Chevrolet and the Taurus. One of the producers motioned his soundman to direct the microphone toward the conversation about P.S. 128.

"Miss Goldhurst," Tepper said. "I'm double-parked here. I'm about to circle the block to look for a spot."

"I'd give you mine, Murray, but I still have forty minutes on the meter. On a schoolteacher's pension, you know, we have to watch every penny."

"Don't even think of it," Tepper said. "You're in a legal spot there. But I was just thinking maybe you'd like to join me while I look. We can catch up, after all these years."

"Excellent idea, Murray," Miss Goldhurst said. She got out of her car, locked it, glared at the television people, and got into the passenger seat of Tepper's Chevy. They pulled away, driving slowly, at what Tepper always thought of as spot-searching speed. In his rearview mirror, Tepper could see several of the television people arguing, presumably about who should move to make room for him.

As Tepper turned the corner and slowly made his way along Ludlow Street, he and his former teacher talked about the old days at P.S. 128—the time Danny Callahan's false beard fell off as he recited the Gettysburg Address before the entire student body, the marathon spelling bee between Katie Palermo and Stanley Gershevsky, the problems that the principal (whom they both referred to formally as Mr. Abbott) had with his false teeth when addressing assemblies, the time Murray's friend Jack nailed Stanley Gershevsky's galoshes to the cloakroom floor. Finally, as they were coming around to Houston Street again, Miss Goldhurst said, "What's your game here, Murray?"

"Game?" Tepper said.

"You were a quiet little boy but a thoughtful little boy," Miss Goldhurst said. "I always thought you understood things you weren't necessarily saying much about. I can't see you just sitting in your car to read the newspaper. You could read the newspaper at home. I think you have something up your sleeve."

"Maybe you overestimated me, Miss Goldhurst," Tepper said. They had come to a halt back at Miss Goldhurst's Ford Taurus. Immediately behind her car, a spot was now available. It was being guarded by a phalanx of television cameramen. One of the television crews had been persuaded to clear a space for Tepper, and its van was now double-parked near the corner. Tepper backed into the spot—rather deftly, he couldn't help thinking.

"I don't think I overestimated you, Murray," Miss Goldhurst said, as she got out of the car. "Anyway, whatever you're up to, watch your tush. And when you see your friend Jack tell him I still don't know how he managed to graduate, considering the mark I gave him in deportment."

No sooner had Tepper pulled into the spot and deposited his quarters in the meter than Victor Hessbaugh appeared, accompanied by the same polite policeman who had come to Tepper's car that night on East Seventy-eighth Street. They stopped Tepper as he turned from the meter.

"We are issuing you this summons, sir," the policeman began, "for being in contravention of the city ordinance against unlicensed demonstrations or exhibitions that could—"

"I'll take that for my client," a small man with a beard said, snatching the summons out of the policeman's hand. "My name is Jeremy Thornton, I am the senior staff attorney for the New York Civil Liberties Union, and I represent Mr. Tepper here, a man you have just ticketed for pulling into a legal parking spot and depositing coins in a parking meter—activities that, until this moment, nobody in the United States of America has ever had any reason to believe were illegal." Thornton spoke in a New York street accent so strong it almost seemed inspired by the old Dead End Kids movies, although, according to what Tepper had read about him in newspapers over the years, he was from an old Episcopalian family and was a graduate not only of Williams College but also of Groton.

"Actually, sir," the sergeant said, "the summons is for—"

"Parking in a legal spot," Thornton interrupted. "And we will ask a federal court to enjoin you from this cockamamie use of an unconstitutional ordinance to punish my client for obeying the law."

"Don't pull any of your civil-liberties flimflam here, Thornton," Victor Hessbaugh said, as the television cameramen pressed closer to catch the exchange. "You know perfectly well that this man's intention—"

"His intention!" Thornton said, at nearly a shout. "His intention! Are we putting law-abiding citizens who have broken no law whatsoever behind bars now for what we believe might be their intentions?"

"Nobody's putting anybody behind bars," Hessbaugh said.

"You got that right, bubbele!" Thornton said. "And I think a federal district judge will be appalled that you tried. What makes you think my client is here to contravene the order against unlicensed demonstrations or exhibitions? What makes you think he isn't in the market for some pickled herring?"

"Actually," Tepper said, "I was going to pick up some herring salad and a whitefish."

"You were?" Thornton said, apparently surprised that his hypothetical point should turn out to be based on fact.

Tepper nodded, and walked into Russ & Daughters. The television cameramen and part of the crowd that had gathered followed him. Irving Saper, by chance, was free, and immediately said, "May I serve you, Mr. Tepper?"

"I'd like a pound of herring salad and a whitefish," Tepper said. The television cameras pushed toward the counter to show Saper scooping out the herring salad. The reporters took notes.

"Any particular whitefish?" Saper said, after he'd put the herring salad in a package and moved down the counter toward the whole fish.

"Whichever one seems appropriate, in your judgment," Tepper said, rather formally. "I'm certain that this store has only nice whitefish in its inventory."

As Tepper emerged from the store, followed by the cameramen and the crowd, he saw that Hessbaugh and the police sergeant had adjourned for a conference a few yards down the street, but two other people had taken their places next to the Chevy Malibu. One was Maxie Allen, dressed in his usual shiny black suit and standing behind an electronic keyboard of the sort you might see used by a trio playing the smaller cocktail lounge of a cruise ship. The other was Bill Carmody, the Woodside Wacko, dressed in blue jeans and a T-shirt that advertised Grain Belt beer and a baseball cap that said on it HEREFORD—THE ALL BEEF BREED. As Tepper approached, Maxie Allen did a few notes of introduction, and then Carmody began to sing.

> *When asked to move by someone from some "burb,"*
> *He said, "Right now this here's my stretch of curb,"*
> *He said it softly. Didn't storm or shout.*
> *He wasn't there to hassle or disturb.*
> *But if you're here to write a little blurb,*
> *Just tell them Tepper isn't going out.*
> *Though he alone knows what it's all about,*
> *Just tell them Tepper isn't going out.*

The crowd that had pushed in on the sidewalk and even out on Houston Street began to chant: *"Tepper isn't going out, Tepper isn't going out. . . ."*

24. *Sunday Lunch*

"THE WHITEFISH IS NOT SO BAD," TEPPER SAID, LATER that morning, as he put another helping of it on his plate. He was sitting at the dining room table of his apartment with his entire family—his wife, his daughter, his son-in-law, and Max, his grandson.

"I've tasted worse," Ruth said. They were accustomed to expressing their approval of food from a delicatessen or an appetizing store—what Tepper sometimes called New York food—in a restrained manner. "Not bad at all" was about as far as they tended to go toward paying a compliment. Tepper had been brought up that way. His father had always seemed reluctant to display excess enthusiasm at the table, particularly when eating New York food—his favorite sort of food. Tepper always suspected that in his father's view if someone exclaimed, "This is absolutely the most spectacular pastrami I've ever tasted in my life!" the Evil Eye would hear what had been said and immediately infuse the pastrami with *E. coli* bacteria.

"I can remember going down to Houston Street to get smoked fish with you when I was still in a car seat, Daddy," Linda said. "It shows some things never change."

"I think they may have changed the rules on the meters," Tepper corrected her. "As I remember, it didn't always say *including* Sunday. But maybe I'm wrong."

"Richard, do you want some whitefish?" Linda asked.

"No, thank you," Richard said, with a quick, tight smile. Richard had never shown himself to be particularly fond of the sort of food the Teppers were likely to serve for Sunday lunch, but he'd always been polite about declining seconds.

"Max, you want some whitefish?" Linda asked, cutting off a piece and offering it to her son, a little boy with impossible blond curls who was sitting next to her.

"Nooooo, thank you," Max said. When offered food he held under suspicion, Max had a way of drawing out the "No" in "No, thank you," so the phrase sounded like the response of someone asked if he'd like to go along for the ride when a new supersonic fighter plane is test-flown for the first time.

"Ruth, look at Max's new tooth," Tepper said.

"What new tooth?" Ruth said. "Maxie doesn't have a new tooth."

As she peered in Max's mouth, Tepper pulled at the top of his fork, which lengthened like a radio antenna until it was nearly two feet long. Then he picked up a piece of whitefish from Ruth's plate. Ruth took no notice of the theft. Max howled with laughter. He never tired of the extendable fork.

Tepper thought the fork was perhaps the only positive thing to have come from his nearly forty years of working with Barney Mittgin, who at one point was trying to sell extendable forks through the mail to people who had sent away for dribbling glasses and hand buzzers. At first, Tepper hadn't believed that it could be one of Mittgin's items, since it seemed to have only one use—eating off other people's plates for the entertainment of small children or the benefit of boorish overeaters. "Not at all," Mittgin had said. "It's also a fork." Seeing Tepper's puzzlement, Mittgin went on: "It does have two uses. It's an extendable fork, but it's also a fork. You can also use it as a fork."

"I was mistaken," Tepper said, with mock innocence, when Ruth had completed her inspection of Max's mouth without finding any new teeth. "Max has no new teeth."

"Here, everybody, have some more herring salad," Ruth said, picking up the plate and starting it around the table. "It's really not bad."

"How did things go down there this morning?" Linda asked her father.

"Oh, fine, once I found a spot," Tepper said. "I got waited on right away. I had a little trouble finding a spot, but the driver of one of the television trucks was nice enough to make room for me."

"There were television trucks?" Linda asked. "Were they there because of you?"

"I suppose they were," Tepper said. "Although I hardly said a word. It was mostly between a lawyer from the city and my lawyer. Well, I suppose he's my lawyer—Jeremy Thornton from the Civil Liberties Union." Tepper thought he heard a sharp intake of breath from his son-in-law at the mention of Thornton's name.

"Daddy," Linda said, "Richard and I . . . well . . ."

"We've been wondering if this hasn't, well, gotten out of hand," Richard said.

There was silence at the table. Finally, Tepper said, "What do you think, Max?"

"Make Grandma look at my teeth again," Max said.

"Daddy, it was one thing when it was sort of private. But now it's in the newspapers all the time. You know a reporter tried to interview Maxie and me. And someone mentioned it to Richard at work last week."

Tepper nodded. Richard worked on Wall Street, trading in something called derivatives. Derivative of what Tepper didn't know. Tepper knew that it wasn't Richard's fault that he made a living doing something his father-in-law didn't understand. He knew it wasn't fair to expect Richard to work in some field that had actually existed when Tepper was a young man. Still, he found himself wondering sometimes whether trading in derivatives was a proper job. He wondered whether people who traded derivatives had as much time on their hands as people who traded commodities. He was aware, of course, that his own father wouldn't have considered brokering mailing lists a proper job.

"Daddy," Linda went on. "We want you to do whatever makes you happy, but can I just ask if you see this as something you'll always do?"

"Always?" Tepper said. "No, I wouldn't think always."

Linda looked relieved. So did Ruth. So did Richard. The silence was broken by Max. "Grandma," he said. "Wanna see my new tooth?"

25. *Shop Talk*

ON A RAINY EVENING A FEW DAYS LATER, TEPPER PULLED into a spot on West Eighty-fourth Street, only a couple of blocks from his apartment. On that side of the street, cars would have to be moved by eight the following morning. Still, the spot he'd found was the only one left. It occurred to him that parking in the area might have become even tighter since he had finally given in to Ruth's entreaties about renting garage space.

It had been years since he'd looked for a spot in his own neighborhood. He didn't even know if Hector, the doorman who had tried to teach him the two fingered whistle, was still working on West Eighty-third, only a block away. For all Tepper knew, Hector had retired by now. He might even have died, taking the secret of his whistling technique with him to the grave. There was a time when Hector had been a significant figure in Tepper's life. Tepper edged the back wheels of the Chevy a bit closer to the curb. He was confident now that he was a perfect two or three inches from the curb, and equidistant from the cars ahead of and behind him. He remembered how he would have felt in those alternate-side days if he'd found the single available spot on a street just after he began looking—a spot that was pretty tight, in fact, too small for a less skilled parker. True, it wasn't good for tomorrow, but he was going to return the car to his garage later in the evening anyway. "Beautiful spot," Tepper mumbled, just loud enough to hear himself. Then he said it in a loud, clear voice: "Beautiful spot!"

A few moments later, he heard a knock on the passenger-side window. A man was standing outside, protecting himself from the rain with a black umbrella.

"Mr. Tepper?" he said.

Tepper leaned over and unlocked the door.

The man closed his umbrella, shook the water off of it, and put it on the floor under the dashboard. Then, as he settled into the passenger seat, he stuck out his hand and said, "Mike Shanahan, Mr. Tepper. Appreciate your taking the time to see me."

"You said on the phone you take surveys, Mr. Shanahan."

"Well, I'm mainly someone who does surveying for politicians, Mr. Tepper."

"You might say we're in related fields—trying to figure out something about people we don't know," Tepper said.

"That's right," Shanahan said.

"Only you try to make your universe as random as possible," Tepper said. "And I try to get rid of all the randomness I can."

Shanahan nodded. "I suppose that's the difference," he said. "Listen, I want to thank you again for meeting me here. I hope it wasn't inconvenient."

"No problem at all, Mr. Shanahan," Tepper replied. "It might have been—I hadn't realized how hard it's gotten to park around here, even on a weeknight; I quit leaving the car on the street some years ago—but, fortunately, I got the last spot on the block. A beautiful spot, really."

"I've often found this a difficult neighborhood to find a spot in," Shanahan said.

"Well, it's harder than some," Tepper said. "I'll tell you the easiest area for parking during the evening; I'm not talking now about good for tomorrow, but just for the evening."

Shanahan held up his hand. "Don't tell me," he said. "The East Side in the seventies, close to the park."

"Exactly," Tepper said. "Exactly. Maybe those people are all rich enough to keep their cars in garages. We have some friends who live on Seventy-third and Madison. They're not rich. They were fortunate enough to be living there in a rent-controlled apartment in the early seventies when the building went co-op, so they picked up their apartment for a song. Anyway, when these friends invite us for dinner, I'm always excited. The food's nothing special, and you might even say the company's only so-so—her brother's often there, and he's one of those people who's always telling you how much his house has appreciated—but the parking is glorious. Sometimes, I'll pull up to their corner, on Madison, and there are four or five spots available at meters that don't need to be fed after seven. I just glide into one of the spots. I take my choice. I always say to my wife, 'Well, I've just had the high point of the evening. No matter what happens, the rest of it will be downhill.'"

"I'm afraid your friends are the sort of people who make it difficult for a poll taker to figure out who he's talking to according to what neighborhood they live in," Mike Shanahan said. "You can't count on, say, the 10021 zip code being all rich people. There are people who lucked onto a co-op first offering. There are people who have been in a rent-controlled apartment for thirty years."

"And," Tepper said, "you can't count on neighborhoods to be reliably poor, either. My partner's niece just paid a fortune for an apartment on Rivington Street. It's considered hip. But you may have known that."

"Sometimes I think that there are people out there who act in weird and unpredictable ways just to complicate the lives of people in our line of work," Shanahan said. "Sometimes I can imagine them out there, purposely living in the wrong neighborhood and voting against their own interests and behaving in ways that everything about them would lead you to believe they would never behave."

Tepper nodded sympathetically. "There's always something," he said.

"It must have been difficult keeping the car on the street and having to move it every day," Shanahan said.

"Well, I was used to it," Tepper said. "I had an old car when we got married, and we just kept it on the street. We wouldn't have had the money for a garage. Also, parking was easier then. My wife's an artist—she does watercolors of fields or beaches or things like that—and we liked driving out of the city on the weekends to someplace she might want to paint. If we were invited to someone's place for dinner and it was farther than walking distance, we'd drive, even if it wasn't on Seventy-third and Madison. If you're keeping your car on the streets, of course, there's a decision there, particularly if you're already in a place that's good for tomorrow. There are a lot of decisions. It's not easy. But as a friend of mine who used to keep his car on the street always said, 'If you want it easy, you could live in Elmira.'"

Shanahan nodded. "It's a tough town, all right," he said.

"Actually, a man who came to see me when I was parked on Houston Street, a man close to my age, told me that he still felt tremendous guilt because when he was a young bachelor in New York he used to rate girls, as we then called young women, according to whether they were worth moving his car for," Tepper said. "He lived in Murray Hill and he kept his car on the street. If one of his friends offered to fix him up with some girl, this fellow would say, 'Is she G.F.T. level?' That meant Good for Tomorrow. In other words, if his car was already parked in a spot that was good for tomorrow, would it be worth giving up the spot to take this particular girl to, say, City Island to eat steamed clams. Now this man has three grown daughters and times have changed and he understands all that and he feels guilty about having had an attitude that he now sees as demeaning to women."

"So what did you tell him?"

"Well, in the first place, I told him that in those years alternate-side parking in Murray Hill was already no picnic."

Shanahan nodded. "So there was nothing frivolous about making that a part of his decision," he said.

"That's right," Tepper said. "Not at all. And also I asked him about meeting the girl he married. It turns out that he met her at a Sunday brunch one of his neighbors was having, at a time when his car was good until the next Thursday, because the parking rules were suspended for some national holiday on Tuesday. But she wanted to go to Coney Island to ride the roller coaster, so he took her. And he knew then that she was the girl he was going to marry. Why else would he have given up that spot? So I reminded him that the G.F.T. system had turned out to have at least one nice result: he was able to realize when he'd met the girl of his dreams. They just celebrated their thirty-fifth anniversary, and he told her that, even after all these years, if she wanted to go somewhere and he had a spot that was good for an entire week because it was one of those years when the Solemnity of the Ascension and Memorial Day and Shavuot all fell just right, he would move his car for her. I thought it was a lovely thing to say, even though, as it happens, he now keeps his car in a garage."

"It's the thought that counts," Shanahan said.

They sat silently for a moment or two, and then Tepper said, "So what is it you wanted to see me about? You weren't very specific on the telephone."

"Well, for the past few years I've been working mainly for Mayor Ducavelli," Shanahan said. "Taking surveys. But in the political business, people who take surveys become advisers. So I've been one of his advisers, really."

"Can I ask you a question about that?"

"Of course."

"Do you go to some of the functions the mayor has in Gracie Mansion?"

"Yes. Now and then."

"That always seemed to me the hardest neighborhood for parking in the whole city," Tepper said. "In the eighties, way over east there. I've logged some circling time over there. So how do you find a spot when you go to one of those functions?"

"Well, actually, I usually take a cab," Shanahan said. "I usually go there straight from the office in a cab."

Tepper nodded. "That neighborhood's a killer," he said. "A killer."

"Anyway," Shanahan went on. "It looks to me like you and the mayor are on a collision course. There are some of us around the mayor who think he's making a big mistake. But I honestly don't think he can help himself. Ironically, even though you seem to be a stickler for obeying the law, he sees you as a sort of advance man for what he thinks of as the forces of disorder."

Tepper nodded. "The mayor hasn't been very complimentary," he said. "Although I've tried to assure my wife that he doesn't mean all those things he says about me personally."

"The mayor sometimes gets carried away when he goes into what we call his attack mode," Shanahan said. "Mr. Tepper, what I think you understand here is that there's no way to stop the mayor from pursuing this collision course. I want to assure you, by the way, that he really had nothing to do with the summons you got for hailing a taxi in the street—that was a total coincidence—but I wouldn't deny that he's capable of that sort of thing. Once he gets on something, he is sort of, well, single-minded. So what I was wondering is whether there's any way to head you off in a slightly different direction. Because if this collision happens, the mayor will cause you as much trouble as he can, but I think he'd be causing himself even more trouble. I happen to think Mayor Ducavelli has been a pretty good mayor. Oh, yes, he's a little paranoid. And a little vindictive. And egotistical. And self-righteous. And stubborn. The man is definitely stubborn. But, all in all, I think he's been good for the city. It's sort of my job to help him get elected again, but I genuinely think his reelection would be a good thing for the city—all in all."

"I'm not sure what you're asking me," Tepper said.

"Well, look, Mr. Tepper. I've been in politics all my life. My father was a precinct captain in Queens. I may talk all sorts of fancy computer-model talk when I present one of the surveys I take, but the sort of politics I understand best is the old-fashioned kind: if we need something from you, we find out what we can do for you. Nothing illegal, of course. Nothing sneaky. Just simple old-fashioned quid pro quo. I know you have a perfect right to park in whatever legal spot you want to park in. What I'm saying is that if you decided you didn't want to do that anymore it would be a great help to us. It would be a great help to the mayor—although, God knows, he has no idea I'm talking to you about this and if he did he'd throw one of his hissy fits."

"So you're saying that if I decided that I was no longer interested in reading the newspaper in my car from time to time, it would be a favor to you and you'd be willing to do me a favor in return."

"Exactly," Shanahan said.

"What favor did you have in mind?"

"Well, Mr. Tepper," Shanahan said. "Frankly, I sort of thought you might have one in mind yourself."

Tepper shook his head. "No," he said.

"I don't suppose you have a nephew who you think might be good in some city job?" Shanahan said. "Or maybe you've got a building permit application that needs a little expediting?"

Tepper shook his head again. "No," he said. "I'm afraid not. I don't have any nephews, and I'm not building anything."

Shanahan nodded. "Well, it was a thought," he finally said.

"It was nice of you to ask, anyway," Tepper said.

Shanahan reached for his umbrella, put his hand on the door handle, and then paused. "Tell me," he said, "I'm curious. If you're trying to sell something that appeals specifically to rich people—let's say one of those rare-wine-of-the-month clubs—do you just send a mailing to everyone in the 10021 zip code anyway and not worry about hitting a lot of not-so-rich people who happen to live there because they have rent-controlled apartments?"

"Well, it's the firms that use what we call horizontal lists who have to be concerned about that," Tepper said. "They start with a sort of master list that essentially includes everybody in the entire country—a list that's created from motor vehicle licenses or telephone directories—and then they chop it up by neighborhoods according to a lot of information that's available from the census on income and median age and all that. We deal with what're called vertical lists. If we're trying to sell people rare wine, we might test a list of, say—"

"People who have subscribed to a magazine for gourmets," Shanahan said.

"Exactly," Tepper said. "Then charge-account customers of fancy glassware stores. Then lists that have to do in some way with backgammon. For some reason, there's a connection between wine snobbery and backgammon playing. There are a lot of odd connections like that in our business."

"You know, I heard a story years ago from somebody in the political trade about a list of people who sent away for this car-cleaning cloth."

"The story is true," Tepper said.

"Best fund-raising list for the Republican National Committee?"

"Democrats, too, if I'm not mistaken."

"You know a lot about this, Mr. Tepper."

"Well, forty years. . . ."

Shanahan nodded again. "I enjoyed our little chat," he said. "Listen, if you are going to continue parking, I might drop around sometime, if you don't mind. I don't mean to talk about you and the mayor—that was just a thought—but just to talk."

"It would be my pleasure," Tepper said.

26. *Hearing*

MURRAY TEPPER TOOK A LEISURELY STROLL FROM THE
subway stop at Bowling Green to the new federal courthouse, an
imposing building not far from the little park that separates the
courthouses of both state and federal government from Chinatown. Tepper's memories of the area were mostly from being on
jury duty. Any number of times over the years, he had walked
across the little park, past the funeral home where an Italian
street band sometimes stood waiting to lead a Chinese funeral,
and into Chinatown for lunch. He often wondered what it was
like being called to jury duty in cities whose courts weren't next
to Chinatown. Once, after Ray Fannon had been on jury duty, he
wrote in his column, "If the time comes when I have to stand
before the bar of justice and be judged by a jury of my peers—if
the time comes, that is, when one Republican too many explains
how much better off we'd all be if the rich paid less in taxes, and
I get violent—I can only hope that the judgment comes in Lower
Manhattan and in the afternoon, after those good citizens serv-
ing as jurors have their bellies full of dumplings and are feeling
so blessed that a little mercy might be in order."

Ruth and Jack and Howard Gordon had all asked Tepper if he
wanted company. He had told them all not to bother. It was, after

all, only a brief hearing on his lawyer's request for a temporary injunction against city officials, to prevent them from prosecuting him under the 1911 ordinance prohibiting unlicensed demonstrations and exhibitions. "As long as the people on the subway don't realize that they're in the presence of an unlicensed exhibition, I think I can make it down there all right by myself," he'd assured them.

As he approached Pearl Street, he heard some chanting, but he couldn't make out the words. Coming closer, he thought he heard his name in the chant. It was, in fact, his name. He could see the demonstrators now, in front of the federal court building. They were marching in a loop on the sidewalk, like strikers picketing their place of employment, and they were chanting, *"Tepper isn't going out, Tepper isn't going out, Tepper isn't going out."* Some of them were holding placards that showed a picture of him in his Chevy under the legend HANDS OFF MURRAY. Standing partway up the stairs was Bill Carmody, dressed in khakis and a T-shirt from an onion festival in South Georgia and a baseball hat from Del's Quik-Stop in Cosgrove, Oklahoma. He was acting as chant leader, waving his arms like the director of a chorale, although the demonstrators—there seemed to be about fifty of them—didn't appear to need much help in keeping up a strong, rhythmic chant.

When the Tepper supporters spotted Tepper himself, they stopped chanting and began cheering. They broke ranks and surged toward him. A few of them wanted to carry him up the stairs and into the building on their shoulders, but he managed to convince them that he actually preferred walking. He politely said "No thank you" to three or four television reporters who jammed a microphone toward him and asked him how he felt. A number of the demonstrators followed him into the building, leaving their signs with those who remained behind. As he entered the front door, Tepper could hear one of those remaining outside explain to a television reporter, "The man's mad as hell. He is mad as hell. . . ."

"No, he's not mad as hell," someone else in the group said. "He's just trying to read the afternoon paper in peace, for Christ's sake. We're the ones who are mad as hell."

Almost every seat in the courtroom was taken, although it was a vast room, much larger than any of the state courtrooms Tepper was familiar with from jury duty. There were microphones both at the witness stand and at the lawyers' tables. Huge windows presented a beautiful view of midtown Manhattan to the north. Jeremy Thornton, the attorney from the Civil Liberties Union, was waiting for Tepper at the defense counsel's table. Tepper started to shake hands, but Thornton grabbed him in a hug instead. Next to Thornton was an efficient looking young woman who was busily going through a small hillock of legal documents on the table in front of her, as if confirming that everything was in its proper order. When Thornton introduced her as his colleague, Eleanor Brown, she said hello to Tepper as quickly as possible and then got back to her documents. Behind her was a sort of supermarket cart filled with more documents. Tepper couldn't imagine how a case that had yet to come to court had already generated so much paper.

As Tepper sat down in the chair Thornton indicated, he noticed Victor Hessbaugh at the next table, accompanied by two or three assistants. Hessbaugh nodded politely. Tepper nodded in return and then turned to Jeremy Thornton, who seemed eager to bring him up-to-date.

"What we got here today, Murray, is a motion for a temporary injunction and a request for a hearing on a permanent injunction," Thornton said. "We ask the judge to keep the city from enforcing this ordinance—the one they used to issue you the summons—while we wait to get on her calendar for a hearing on a permanent injunction. We like to come prepared, which is why Eleanor here has a cart that makes her look like she's about to hit the checkout counter at Balducci's on the day before Thanksgiving, but, if everything goes the way it usually goes, this shouldn't be complicated."

The clerk of the court stood, and the audience in the courtroom became quiet. "All rise," the clerk said. "The United States District Court for the Southern District of New York is now in session, Judge Lorraine Bernardi presiding."

Everyone stood for the entrance of the judge—a handsome woman in her late forties, with dark hair shading to gray. She sat down, and, at a signal from the clerk, the others in the courtroom sat down as well. Judge Bernardi looked down at those gathered at the counsel tables before her. She said good morning and then said, "Well, Mr. Thornton, it looks like you're up."

"Thank you, Your Honor," Thornton said, rising to speak. "What we're asking here, on behalf of my client, Mr. Murray Tepper, who is seated here next to me, is a temporary injunction to prevent the city of New York from enforcing, in a completely arbitrary and capricious manner, this ordinance—which is supposedly on the books for the purpose of keeping order but is, if I may say so, so broadly drawn as to be virtually meaningless—

against Mr. Tepper, who has, in fact, broken no law, city, state, or federal."

"If I may, Your Honor," Victor Hessbaugh said when the judge looked his way. "Mr. Tepper was given a citation on East Seventy-eighth Street, following an incident on Houston Street in which his presence caused a serious altercation. Then he purposely returned to Houston Street—"

"As part of a conspiracy to buy herring salad," Thornton interjected.

"Mr. Thornton," the judge said sternly. "You will wait to be recognized by the court before you speak."

"I'm sorry, Your Honor," Thornton said.

"Thank you, Your Honor," Hessbaugh said. "Your Honor, the city has a responsibility to keep order on its own streets, and would strongly oppose this motion. I would be happy to outline in detail the precedents in law for this ordinance at the court's convenience."

Judge Bernardi studied the documents before her for a few moments. Finally, she said, "Exactly where on Seventy-eighth Street, Mr. Tepper?"

It took Tepper a moment to realize he was being addressed directly by the judge, and then he said, "Between Lexington and Park, Your Honor."

The judge smiled slightly and nodded. "I used to look for spots in that area myself some years ago," she said. "When I stayed home with my children for a few years, before going back into practice, it was my task to move the family car from one side of the street to another. I used to go fifteen or twenty minutes early to the side that would be okay the next morning, and read law journals until it was safe to leave the car. Tell me, is it difficult to park around there these days?"

"I would say that parking for the evening is not a problem, Your Honor, but parking so that you're good for tomorrow is not an easy task," Tepper said.

"Still a lot of Diplomatic Plates Only in that area?"

"Yes, Your Honor," Tepper said. "I'm afraid there are still a lot of spaces taken from the public and reserved for diplomatic plates."

Judge Bernardi nodded slowly, as if Tepper's information had confirmed what she'd expected to hear. The two lawyers, who were still standing, glanced around, as if for some signal about what they were supposed to do. Finally, the judge said, "Well, gentlemen, the first time I can hear you present your arguments in this matter in the full detail for which you are both justly known is four weeks from today. Let me ask you something, Mr. Tepper."

"Yes, Your Honor," Tepper said.

"I'm going to grant this temporary injunction," the judge said. "But I am a little concerned about the potential for disturbance the city attorney has mentioned. People feel strongly about this issue, as we can see from the demonstrators in front of the building. We're getting into summer. It's hot. Tempers sometimes are short, particularly among people who have been circling for a spot and find nothing but Diplomatic Plates Only signs. I wonder how you would feel about—in a strictly voluntary way, without jeopardizing any of your rights here—not parking in some of these places—Seventy-eighth Street, Houston Street, et cetera—until we have our hearing."

"Your Honor—" Jeremy Thornton began.

"It would be my pleasure, Your Honor," Tepper said.

"Thank you, Mr. Tepper," the judge said. "I appreciate that. The restraining order is granted. The motion on the permanent injunction will be held four weeks from today, gentlemen. Nine o'clock. See you then."

27. *Family Decision*

"MURRAY," RUTH SAID. IT WAS NOT ONE OF THE MURRAYS she used for "Murray, pass the salt." Tepper had just returned to the dinner table after taking a telephone call from Sy Lambert, who was phoning daily now with details about his plans for what he liked to call the Murray Tepper Money Machine. Lambert had just called to report on a conversation he'd had with Jeffrey Green, the young man who first interviewed Tepper, about the possibility of being the ghostwriter for the book of advice that would launch Tepper as an author. Tepper had said that for a young man who dreamt of being a political reporter, ghosting an advice book—or, really, a series of advice books if Lambert's plans worked out—might represent a serious career deflection. "That's just what he said," Lambert had replied. "But after the figure I mentioned, he asked for some time to think about it." Then Lambert had launched into a speech on the glories of subsidiary rights.

"Murray," Ruth repeated, and Tepper realized he hadn't replied.

"Yes, Ruth," he said.

"Murray, you're not very comfortable with this Lambert, are you?" Ruth said.

"Well, he's what my father would have called a big shot, or a *k'nocker*," Tepper said. "He likes to boast about his art collection and his house in East Hampton. He likes to drop the names of the important people he knows. Tonight, he told me a story so he could mention his latest visit with a famous bullfighter. He seemed disappointed that I hadn't heard of the bullfighter, although I tried to explain to him that I don't follow bullfighting closely. It's true that Sy Lambert is not the sort of person I would ordinarily know. But I feel that our acquaintanceship will be only temporary."

"Even if there's a series of books?" Ruth asked.

"Oh, he seemed amused that I thought my participation would be necessary for the series of books," Murray said. "He said, 'Murray, I told you: that's just content and the author doesn't have to worry about content.'"

"Murray," Ruth said, in a tone that told him they hadn't arrived at the real subject of the conversation yet. "I feel that you're getting involved in some of these things—some things with this Lambert, for instance—for my sake."

"For your sake?"

"Because you want to make sure we have enough for retirement, and maybe because you're thinking that if it all happens we'll be able to get the cottage in the West of England after all, so I can paint."

Tepper was pondering how to answer that when the telephone rang again.

"Touch?" a voice said, when Tepper picked up the receiver and said hello. "It's me, Touch—Barney Mittgin."

"I know," Tepper said. Nobody else in the world called him Touch.

"Sorry to bother you at home," Mittgin said, "but I wanted to alert you that I'm going to be on the eleven o'clock news tonight. Channel Seven. They already interviewed me. On tape."

"Are you declaring for Congress?" Tepper said.

"Declaring for Congress?" Mittgin said, puzzled. "No, I'm talking about you. With the hearing coming up, they're doing a piece about what they call the Tepper Affair. You're an affair now. Like the Dreyfus Affair. The Tepper Affair. Of course, the Tepper Affair is partly the Mittgin Affair, because I'm moving some of my airplane pillows. They taped a pretty long interview with me. I don't know how much they'll use. I hope they use the part where I say that you're a symbol of the alienation of our times."

"I am?" Tepper said.

"Well, it's more like a metaphor," Mittgin said. "It doesn't mean you personally. I heard a lecture about it. It turns out that almost everything is a symbol of the alienation of our times. You'll like what I said. Also, it might sell a few pillows."

Tepper told Mittgin that he and Ruth were in the middle of dinner but that they'd certainly watch Channel Seven at eleven, if they were still awake.

"Murray," Ruth said, when he'd returned. "I just want you to know that it's not important to me. I mean, I'd love to have the cottage and to have enough now for our retirement so we don't have to worry, but I think we're fine. You still enjoy work. Linda's taken care of, from whatever those things are that Richard sells. The cottage would be nice, but I'm not sure that I want to be that far from Maxie anyway, even for part of the year. I don't want you to get involved in something you're not comfortable with, just for my sake."

Tepper nodded. "I think everything will work out," he said.

28. *Options*

"MISS GOLDHURST REALLY SAID THAT ABOUT MY MARK in deportment?" Jack said. "What a fine memory that old bird has. She must have been thinking of the unfortunate incident concerning Stanley Gershevsky's galoshes, where I believe I was only performing a public service. As you may remember, when the last bell rang, Stanley would go into the cloakroom, step right into his galoshes, and walk away, without even breaking stride— his only cool move."

They were at their usual table at the Japanese restaurant for lunch. "I was having trouble remembering that," Tepper said, pouring them both a cup of tea. "You glued them to the floor?"

"I believe that gluing would have produced what our shop teacher, Mr. Inman, of blessed memory, called a halfway job," Jack said. "I nailed them. How did I manage to swing the hammer inside the galosh, you may ask. I didn't. I utilized a piece of lead pipe filled with concrete, which I'd fortuitously come across in the vacant lot next to Stinky Weinberg's building. I placed one end on the nails and I hammered on the other end from above Stanley Gershevsky's galoshes. The result was what Mr. Inman would have called a good, clean job. I hated Stanley Gershevsky."

At last, the scene flashed into Tepper's head: the vile Stanley

Gershevsky, doing his one cool move by stepping into his galoshes without breaking stride and falling on his face in the boys' cloakroom.

The waitress approached to take their orders. "Two regular sushi specials," Jack said. "And two beers."

The waitress wrote that down, and continued to stand in front of the table. Jack said nothing more. Finally, she said, "Mee-dyum wher-ah?" and burst into a giggle.

"No. Raw, please," Jack said. "And, by the way, can you get gefilte fish on the regular sushi special, or would that be an extra charge?"

The waitress looked puzzled.

"Just two regular sushi specials and two beers," Tepper said.

When the waitress left, Jack said, "So let me get this straight. When you were in court a few weeks ago, the judge said she would hear the arguments on the injunction in a month."

"Right," Tepper said. "Next Thursday, at nine o'clock."

"And meanwhile you have suspended your front-seat therapy sessions and outdoor newspaper reading, as a courtesy to the judge, who's a sort of soul mate of yours since she used to do alternate-side parking in the East Seventies."

"That's right," Tepper said. "Now she has a garage."

"And this guy Shanahan has hinted that if you decided sitting in a parked car in a legal spot wasn't that exciting after all, somebody in City Hall could see to it that you get a zoning variance in case you want to run an auto-body-repair shop in your apartment or something like that."

"Right."

"But if, instead, you do continue to park around in the evenings and the mayor attempts to crush you like a bug," Jack went on, "you become famous, so that Sy Lambert can market you like a folk hero, a sort of stationary Charles Lindbergh."

"That's right, too," Tepper said. "According to this proposal he's sent me, it would start with a book—*From the Front Seat* he wants to call it. The format would be like an advice column in the newspapers."

"I take it Murray Tepper would offer simple but profound advice on a wide array of problems," Jack said. "Personal problems, philosophical problems, dermatological problems."

"You've got it," Tepper said.

"There's enough advice for a book?"

"I asked him that," Tepper said. "He says there's always enough anything for a book. With a book, he says, what counts is that it's about or by somebody famous. In fact, he sees *From the Front Seat* being followed by *More From the Front Seat*, then *Still More From the Front Seat*. Apparently, an advice book by a famous person is like a cookbook by a famous person. You can always find advice, the way you can always find recipes. Anyway, he says that once the book series gets going, you expand with speaking tours, plus what they call ancillary products."

"I have a great idea for a product," Jack said. "A Murray Tepper windup toy. It's a Chevy with a guy at the wheel, and when you wind it up it doesn't go anywhere."

"I think that audiotapes are more the sort of thing he had in mind," Tepper said. "Plus the movie, of course. He talks a lot about the movie."

"And then, according to the plan, you would have enough money to retire, and maybe even live part of the year in a nice little cottage, near some nice little English fishing shacks."

"Did I already tell you about the cottage?" Tepper asked.

"Ruth told me," Jack said. "We were having a little chat about dream retirements."

"Well, that would be nice," Tepper said.

The waiter arrived with their sushi, and, almost right behind her, Alan Harris suddenly stood, somewhat awkwardly, in front of the table. He had apparently just finished lunch and had spotted Tepper on the way out. "Hello, Mr. Tepper," he said. "I don't want to bother you in the middle of your lunch. I just want you to know that your advice about my little situation was wonderful advice. I think my wife is confident now about how much I truly value what she does, and I just wanted to thank you for your help."

"My pleasure," Tepper said.

"I've been having some nightmares about serpents," Harris said. "But I'm sure that's just temporary."

"I would think so," Tepper said.

"And, if you've got just another second," Harris said. "I wonder if you're going to be at Seventy-eighth Street again anytime soon. A couple of the people I work with would really like to meet you."

"It's a little up in the air now," Tepper said.

"I understand, I understand," Harris said. "Well, I'll just wait to see. Thanks again for your help."

Tepper nodded, and Harris left.

"What were we saying?" Tepper said.

"You were about to tell me about the astonishingly drafty English retirement cottage you're thinking you could buy if the mayor continues to play his role as bully to a folk hero and Sy Lambert arranges for you to cash in," Jack said. "And I was about to guess that you have mixed feelings about signing on with Sy

Lambert, only partly because he's a blowhard. Mainly it's because you find all that stuff a little embarrassing and you're afraid that Linda and her husband, the derivatives man, would find it even more embarrassing. And maybe even Ruth would find it embarrassing. And then your only friend in the family would be Max, who will remain your friend as long as you have your extendable fork, or he grows up."

"Actually," Tepper said, "that's a very good analysis of the situation."

"You forget, Murray: I was always a good student. It was only deportment that was my problem."

29. *Day in Court*

THIS TIME THE COURTHOUSE HAD BEEN SURROUNDED
with the blue wooden sawhorse barriers used by the New York
Police Department for keeping onlookers in their place. Policemen were stationed every fifteen or twenty feet behind the
barriers, and three or four mounted policemen, wearing blue
helmets and long riding boots, patrolled slowly up and down the
street on horseback. Although it was an hour before the hearing,
the crowd was already large. The people in the crowd seemed
relatively good-humored, although the chant that started up now
and then had a strong, almost militant beat: *"Tepper isn't going
out, Tepper isn't going out, Tepper isn't going out."* Vendors with
carts were taking advantage of the occasion to do a steady business in soft drinks and Italian sausage sandwiches and Sno-
Kones. Tepper thought he recognized the fruit vendor he used to
see on Forty-third Street, but he couldn't be sure.

Ruth had insisted on accompanying her husband to the
hearing. She was holding Tepper's arm as they approached the
courthouse in the middle of a tight little group that also included
Jeremy Thornton and Eleanor Brown, who was pushing her grocery cart full of documents. As the crowd began to chant, Tepper

could feel Ruth's hand tighten on his arm, and he patted it. "They're on our side, dear," he said.

At a break in the barriers, a policeman was checking all those who wanted to enter, making certain that they had business in the courthouse. He waved their party through, directing Eleanor Brown to the ramp for the disabled, where she'd be able to take in her grocery cart without trying to bump it up the stairs. As they passed, Tepper was certain that he heard the policeman mutter, "Give 'em hell, Murray."

After waiting for a while in an attorneys' conference room, Tepper's party was escorted to the courtroom by a court officer. In the hall they passed a long line of people waiting for whatever seats might become available. A seat in the front row had been reserved for Ruth; otherwise there wouldn't have been room for her. The courtroom was jammed. Victor Hessbaugh and two assistants sat at the table for opposing counsel. As Tepper and Thornton and Eleanor Brown passed, Hessbaugh nodded politely.

Thornton and Hessbaugh had both submitted thick briefs to Judge Bernardi, and she announced from the bench that she didn't need to hear every argument repeated in detail. Thornton presented a sort of summary of his brief, stressing the undisputed fact that Murray Tepper, a law-abiding citizen, had been given a summons while specifically obeying the law—parking in an alternate-side spot while parking was permitted, parking at a metered spot while the meter showed parking time had been duly paid for. "Thornton was being uncharacteristically restrained," Ray Fannon later wrote. "It took him a full ten minutes to get to the Magna Carta, although he had made stops at the

Articles of Confederation, the Constitution of the United States, and the European Charter of Rights along the way. There was some betting in the press gallery that Thornton might make it all the way through his speech without comparing Murray Tepper's being told to move from Houston Street with Rosa Parks's being told to move from the front of the bus in Montgomery. Those betting that way, of course, eventually lost their money."

Hessbaugh reminded the court that his brief contained statistics showing that several hundred jurisdictions had ordinances similar to or even precisely the same as the one Murray Tepper was cited under. He spoke at length about the duty of the mayor and the police department to keep order in the city for the protection of citizens. He called to the stand an elderly woman who recounted how frightened she had been when she emerged from her weekly trip to Russ & Daughters, clutching a quarter of a pound of Nova Scotia and a quarter of a pound of cream cheese with chives and two sesame bagels, only to find herself in the midst of what she kept referring to as "a big *tsimiss*." He also put on the stand a police officer named Abel Becker who said he'd injured his back in the Seventy-eighth Street altercation—although the testimony was undercut in cross-examination when Thornton, reaching back now and then to be handed a document from the grocery cart by Eleanor Brown, demonstrated that Officer Becker tended to hurt his back with remarkable regularity and was known by some in the department as Bum Back Becker.

Murray Tepper took the stand to testify briefly on direct examination about exactly where and when he had parked his Chevrolet. During Hessbaugh's cross-examination, the questions those in the courtroom were most interested in hearing the witness answer—the questions having to do with why he chose to read the newspaper in a parked car rather than in an easy chair in his own living room—were consistently blocked by objections. Thornton would rise and give some variation of the same speech: "Your Honor, I must object. In this country, under this constitution, it is none of Mr. Hessbaugh's business where Mr. Tepper reads the newspaper or which newspaper he reads or how he spends the rest of his leisure time, as long as Mr. Tepper is within the law. Neither is it the business of the mayor or of the police department or—and I say this with great respect—of this court."

Hessbaugh was reduced to probing for minor parking violations. "Mr. Tepper," he asked at one point, "did you ever—if you were in the middle of an interesting story in the paper or perhaps an interesting conversation with somebody who dropped in to talk to you while you were parking—notice that the meter had run out and therefore go out and put more money in the meter?"

"You mean that, for example, it's a one-hour meter and I've already put enough money in for one hour but the hour is up, do I go put in more money to get maybe another hour?"

"Exactly."

"But Mr. Hessbaugh," Tepper said, in a voice that everyone in the courtroom took as expressing genuine shock. "Feeding the meter past the allotted time is against the law."

Judge Bernardi did not have to go to her chambers to consider the decision. She granted the permanent injunction. Hessbaugh, to no one's surprise, said he would appeal. Judge Bernardi turned to Murray Tepper. "Mr. Tepper," she said. "Again we have a situation where you're perfectly within your rights to resume the activity that brought us all here today, and I will not enjoin you from doing so. However, given the circumstances, I wonder if I could ask you once more to wait to resume parking, purely voluntarily. If so, I would, for my part, do everything I could to see to it that the appeal process is expedited, which could mean a delay in your activity of as little as two or three weeks."

"Your Honor," Tepper said, "it would be my pleasure."

30. *The List*

ON A TUESDAY, TWO WEEKS AFTER JUDGE BERNARDI granted a permanent injunction preventing the city from using the unlicensed-demonstrations ordinance to keep Murray Tepper from parking in a legal spot, Tepper arrived at Worldwide Lists an hour later than usual. At home that morning, he'd had two calls from reporters who wanted to know whether he was going to resume parking if, as expected, the circuit court turned down Victor Hessbaugh's appeal. Jeffrey Green had phoned to discuss the pros and cons of putting his plans for political reporting aside to become a ghostwriter. There had also been a call from Tim Singer, the young man who published *Beautiful Spot: A Magazine of Parking*. Tepper and Singer had become acquainted around the time of the first altercation on Houston Street, when Singer phoned to announce that *Beautiful Spot* was planning to put Tepper on the cover as Parker of the Decade. Mainly because of the publicity surrounding the mayor's attempt to ban its sale in city-owned buildings, *Beautiful Spot* was making great strides in both circulation and advertising revenue. Singer wanted to talk to Murray Tepper again about whether a magazine that had spoken so contemptuously about parkers who were tempted to "sell out to the garage interests" could accept advertising from parking garages without, as Singer put it, "doing violence to our entire raison d'être."

In the weeks that Tepper had been, as the tabloids tended to put it, "off the street," honoring Judge Bernardi's request to suspend his parking forays voluntarily, interest from reporters and agents and entrepreneurs had only grown. The day before, Tepper had heard from a couple of agents who wanted to represent him and from a man who had an Internet site he wanted Tepper to endorse—a site that, for a small subscription fee, would give a member access to the parking regulations on every street in the five boroughs plus information on special holiday parking rules, techniques for fighting parking tickets, and the leading body shops for bumper repair in each borough. Sy Lambert called constantly, outlining new permutations of the Murray Tepper Money Machine and impressing upon Tepper the necessity of striking while the iron was hot. The letters and phone calls and e-mails of support continued to flow in. Somebody had started a website called Tepperisntgoingout.com and was forwarding literally thousands of e-mails on to Worldwide Lists.

When Tepper finally walked into his office, he found Howard Gordon and Arnie Sarnow waiting for him, sitting at the table that was, as usual, strewn with rate cards. "Gentlemen," he said, as he removed his coat and hung it on a hanger on the back of his office door. "Are we having a meeting?"

Sarnow and Gordon remained silent. They looked across the table as each waited for the other to begin speaking. Then Tepper looked more closely at Howard Gordon.

"Howard?" Tepper said. "Do my eyes deceive me, or are you smiling?"

Gordon shrugged, as if modestly taking in a compliment, and his grin grew wider.

"Don't tell me," Tepper said. "You have finally figured out why the list of people who buy the nose-hair-clipping device is the best list for Kiplinger's newsletter."

"No, that's not it," Gordon said, still miraculously smiling. "You tell him, Arnie."

"Murray," Arnie Sarnow said, rather formally, "it gives me great pleasure to inform you that your list is the magic list."

"My list?" Tepper said. "What do you mean by my list?"

"The list of people who wrote or e-mailed their support," Arnie said. "You told me to do a Taunton test on it. Remember? Well, I did. The Taunton people were bowled over. They'd never had results like this since they started doing tests. So they did more tests. And we kept adding names, of course. You were in the middle of this law case, and Howard and I decided I shouldn't distract you with this until I was absolutely sure. So now I'm sure. These people will buy anything. They'll buy life insurance. They'll buy scuba lessons. They'll buy nonstick cook ware. I wouldn't be surprised to hear that they would buy Barney Mittgin's map-pillow."

"I can't believe it," Tepper said.

"Here's the report," Arnie said, picking a thick document off the scattering of rate cards on the table and leafing through it as he spoke. "It's all here. They'll buy genealogical charts. They'll buy the jelly bean of the month. The Taunton people have had time to do two of their extrapolations, and the results are nearly as strong." What the Taunton company called an extrapolation was a way of extending the numbers of a list by analyzing the people on the list according to measurements such as age and median income—measurements available from the fine dicing of census tract information—and then extending the list with people who seemed similar. If extrapolations worked, the size of the list could be tripled or quadrupled in fairly short order.

"But I don't understand," Tepper said. "What's the connection?"

"What's the connection between accountants and designer jeans?" Howard Gordon said. "What's the connection between the nose-hair clipper and the newsletter? Who knows? The connection doesn't make the difference. The percentage of return makes the difference. The percentage of return makes this list a gold mine. That's already obvious from the calls."

"We've had calls?" Tepper asked.

"Apparently, somebody at Taunton must have talked," Gordon said. "I got a couple of calls late yesterday from people who said they heard we got some special magic list. More important, the first thing this morning—half an hour ago—I got a call from a lawyer who specializes in mergers and acquisitions who said he just wondered if Worldwide Lists is in play."

"In play?" Tepper asked.

"In play," Gordon said, somehow smiling even more broadly. "I told him that maybe it was in play and maybe it wasn't in play. It depends. That answer seemed to make him happy. He said he'd talk to his principals and be back to me."

"His principals?"

"His principals."

"And what did you say about your principals?"

"Murray," Howard Gordon said. "You and I own Worldwide Lists, Inc. We *are* our principals."

Gordon and Sarnow looked at Murray Tepper closely, as if waiting for a response that hadn't yet appeared. Finally, Arnie Sarnow said, "Murray, this is it. This is the jackpot. What's the matter?"

"I just hadn't thought of that list in exactly this way," Tepper said. "These people wrote in to support me. Do you think it's all right to rent out their names?"

"But Murray, renting out names is what we do," Howard Gordon said. "That's the business we're in. This is America. If you've got something you can sell and it's legal, you sell it. We live in a . . . what do you call it?"

"A free-market economy," Tepper said, nodding. "I suppose you're right. We live in a free-market economy."

31. *Response*

EXACTLY A WEEK LATER, THE UNITED STATES CIRCUIT
Court of Appeals rather brusquely dismissed the city's appeal of
Judge Bernardi's permanent injunction against using the 1911
peace ordinance to cite Murray Tepper when he parked in a legal
spot. The judges declined even to schedule a hearing on the matter. Mayor Frank Ducavelli responded to that decision by holding an impromptu press conference on the steps of City Hall—a
press conference that proved difficult for City Hall reporters,
since the concertina barbed wire that had begun on the lawn was
now crawling up the steps, like a vine that threatened to take
over, and this greatly limited space close enough to the mayor to
hear what he was saying. There was some disagreement among
the press, in fact, over whether Ducavelli had used the word
"screwy" or "phooey" when discussing the decision, although
everyone heard him say clearly that the judges of the United
States Circuit Court of Appeals were "a bunch of crazies." As
soon as the press conference was over, Mayor Ducavelli had
informed Victor Hessbaugh and Mike Shanahan that they were
expected in an hour to discuss the legal and political implica-
tions of the decision.

"Okay, strap me in," Shanahan said to Teresa as he entered the mayor's outer office, passed successfully through the iris scanner, and walked toward the Body Orifice Security Scanner.

"Listen, I've been thinking about it," Teresa said. "I'm sorry I embarrassed you that time about your retainer."

"It's all right," Shanahan said. "You're entitled. Should I just sit down in this thing?"

"Don't bother," Teresa said. "He's expecting you, and Yesboss is already in there."

"How do you know that I haven't secreted in one of my body orifices a tiny penknife with which I intend to carve out the mayor's gizzard?" Shanahan said.

"I trust you. Also, the mayor was born without a gizzard."

When Shanahan entered, the mayor was pacing in front of his desk. Victor Hessbaugh sat facing him. After a few seconds, the mayor suddenly quit pacing, as if he'd run up against an idea so powerful that it had stopped him in his tracks. "Loitering!" he almost shouted at Hessbaugh. "We'll get him for loitering. Maybe aggravated loitering."

"Well, I could go back over some of the nineteenth-century ordinances," Hessbaugh said. "But I think there's a problem with loitering. If you can arrest somebody for loitering in his own car, then it sort of follows that you can arrest somebody for loitering in his own house. I think we'd have even stronger constitutional problems using a loitering ordinance than we had with the ordinance they just kept us from using."

"The man's a menace," Ducavelli said. He had started pacing again. Shanahan, whose presence still hadn't been acknowledged, sat down next to Hessbaugh.

"As your legal adviser, Mayor, I have to tell you that some of the things you said about Murray Tepper on the steps this morning are probably actionable," Hessbaugh said. "We could argue that he is now a public figure, which makes it harder for him to sue for libel, and I suppose you could claim that it was fair comment to call him an agitator. But Trotskyite?"

"A menace," the mayor repeated. "The man's a menace." He looked over at Mike Shanahan and said, "What do the numbers look like?"

"Well, again, the long and short of it, Mayor, is that you were a lot better off attacking Ukrainians," Shanahan said. "It's been about two months since you first took notice of Murray Tepper— that was when you were in Phoenix and you called him a 'leech on the body politic'—and your approval rating has fallen six points in those two months."

"What did I tell you!" Ducavelli said. "The man's out to destroy me."

"Right now," Shanahan continued, "your head-to-head against Carmody—who, as you know, has gone out of his way to identify himself with Tepper—gives you a lead of fifty-two to forty-eight, which is getting near the margin of error."

"And you think this is from Tepper?"

"He's a very popular man in this city. In fact, when his name is on a survey question, a lot of people actually say that they'd like to see him run for mayor himself."

"So how do you suggest that I handle this Tepper problem?"

"By not calling attention to it, Mayor," Shanahan said. "When you call attention to Murray Tepper, you just play into the hands of the Wacko. On this issue, I would counsel a sustained period of inertness."

The mayor went behind his desk and sat down. He seemed to be considering the possibility of accepting that advice, although it was also possible that he was simply building up steam for an explosion. "Parking is the key to urban order, and I can't seem to get parking under control," he finally said, in a calm voice. Shanahan had never before heard the mayor acknowledge that there was anything he couldn't control. "I haven't been able to figure out how to nail the Ukrainians," the mayor went on. "And now this Tepper has been able to flout my authority with impunity." Then the mayor fell silent.

Shanahan nodded. "There's always something," he said.

32. *Packing Up*

"COME RIGHT IN, MR. FANNON," TEPPER SAID, HOLDING open the apartment door. "It's nice to meet you. I've read your column for many years."

"Sometimes while sitting behind the wheel of a parked car, I hope," Ray Fannon said, extending his hand as he entered the Teppers' apartment.

"Oh, yes, indeed, many times while sitting behind the wheel of a parked car."

Tepper led Fannon into the living room, showed him to a chair, and asked him if he'd like something to drink.

"Oh, no thanks," Fannon said, getting his notebook out of the side pocket of his suit jacket. "I won't take much of your time. I see you're packing."

"Yes, we're going to England for a while," Tepper said, waving toward a couple of suitcases in the hall. "We're hoping to find a cottage there for part of the year, now that I don't have any more business responsibilities."

"Then the sale of Worldwide Lists doesn't entail you and your partner staying on to run it for a period of time?"

"Oh no. They're going to give Arnie Sarnow a chance at that. I suspect it'll work out. He's an intelligent young man, and he's a little more up-to-date than my partner and I are. The development of the list that the purchasers were interested in was really Arnie's work. My partner and I decided that we were ready to retire."

"And no series of advice manuals? No speaking tour?"

"No," Tepper said. "I decided that wasn't for me. Mr. Lambert was disappointed. He said fame was fleeting. But I told him that, as they say in England, I was glad to see the back of it. Actually, you're the first newspaperman I've heard from in quite a while. There was a lot of press interest after the city's appeal was rejected and the mayor called the appeals judges all those names. That next Sunday, when I was free to park again, there were so many people waiting for me on Houston Street that I actually did feel that I could be the cause of a disturbance. You might say I started sympathizing a little with Mr. Hessbaugh's argument, after the fact. The police were very nice about controlling the crowd, but having so many people there, all of them knowing what was supposed to happen, made it all seem less, well, natural. So I didn't go back."

"Well, the point had been made," Fannon said. "I'm not saying that making a point was what you were trying to do, but the point had been made. You showed Il Duce that you couldn't be bullied."

Tepper shrugged and said, "I suppose."

"And, if I might ask, where will your car be while you're in England?"

"Oh, I sold the car," Tepper said.

It took Fannon a couple of moments to register that. Finally, he said, "That must have been difficult. You've been driving a car around the city for a long time. You're the only person I know of who managed to turn parking into a sort of—what shall I say?—philosophy."

"Well, things move on. Years ago, I didn't think I could ever give up alternate-side parking and keep my car in a garage, but I did. Now I find I can give up my car altogether. If we're going to be here only part of the year, it really doesn't make sense. We can always rent a car if we want to go to the country."

For another ten or fifteen minutes, Fannon asked more questions—questions about the legal case, questions about where the Teppers intended to go in England, questions about the meaning of the entire episode. ("I was in a legal spot," Tepper responded to those. "I was always in a legal spot.") Then, putting his notebook back in his pocket, Fannon got up to go. "You know," he said, as Tepper also stood up, "now that I've seen you up close I'm pretty sure I saw you near the beginning of all this. On Seventy-eighth Street. Reading the paper in a parked car."

"Well, Seventy-eighth Street was where I got one of my citations."

"No, I saw that, too. But I mean even before that. One night, as I showed people out of my house after a poker game. It's been bothering me since all of this started. There was a man parked, reading the *Post*, and I think it was you."

Tepper shrugged. "It's possible," he said. "I often parked in that neighborhood."

"Not just in that neighborhood, but on that particular street," Fannon said. "And it finally dawned on me that it might not be a coincidence that Seventy-eighth Street is the street you parked on more than once and is also the home of the columnist who, if I may be so immodest as to say so, has most relentlessly used his column to make underhanded, snide, disrespectful, and maybe even unfair comments about the mayor. So I got out all the newspaper stories and made a list of every parking spot of yours mentioned. I found an interesting pattern. I mean, not a pattern that proves anything. And maybe it's just a coincidence. But on Forty-third Street, you often parked close to the Century Club, where a lot of people who work for places like *The New York Times* and *The New Yorker* show up regularly. Russ & Daughters, on Houston Street, also attracts a certain number of media people. And then you would occasionally park way over on West Fifty-seventh, which turns out to be the block right across from CBS television news. And one of your places was Cooper Square, pretty far downtown from the other spots—a little out of your area, one would think. You did used to park some times on Cooper Square, right?"

"That's right," Tepper said. "It's No Parking, seven to seven, on the west side of the street, but I'd park at the meters on the east side."

"I'm sure you're correct about that," Fannon said. "But what is also interesting about Cooper Square is that's where the office of *The Village Voice* is. What I'm getting at, Mr. Tepper, is if you put all of these spots together a certain pattern emerges. A cynical person could come to the conclusion that, given where you chose to park, if Jeffrey Green hadn't found you, somebody else would have. In other words, that Murray Tepper may be not someone who happened to come to attention and therefore became a folk hero but someone who decided to become a folk hero and therefore came to attention. Maybe in order to cash in on his fame and finance his retirement. And maybe the discovery of the magic list made cashing in unnecessary. What would you think of that theory?"

"Well," Tepper replied. "As you say, the person who came to that conclusion would have to be very cynical."

"True," Fannon said. "And also very embarrassed if he also happened to be the person who wrote with great assurance in a column that Murray Tepper, unlike all the strivers and hustlers in this town, simply wanted to be left alone."

"Well, it may be immodest of me, but I admired that column you wrote about me, Mr. Fannon," Tepper said.

"And I admire you, Mr. Tepper," Fannon said. "Either way. Have a safe trip."

33. *Flight*

THEY WERE SITTING AT ONE OF THE TABLES NEAR A snack bar at JFK, an hour before the morning flight to London was scheduled to take off. Murray and Ruth Tepper were having coffee. Linda was eating a bagel with cream cheese. Max was taking occasional sips of apple juice through a straw.

"Grandma, look at my new teeth," Max said, pulling at Ruth's sleeve but looking conspiratorially at Murray Tepper as he talked.

"Maxie, Grandma's not eating anything," Tepper said, in a loud whisper.

"Eat something, Grandma," Max said. "So you'll grow up strong."

Ruth pulled over Linda's plate and had a bite of the bagel. Then she looked at Max, who had his mouth wide open. "I don't see any new teeth," she said.

Tepper pulled out his extendable fork, reached over to stab half of the bagel, and lifted it from the plate. Max started giggling.

"Didn't you always used to take the overnight flight?" Linda said.

"I decided that I like to see where I'm going," Tepper said.

"Daddy, I think the pilot's the one who has to see where he's going."

"If we're both keeping an eye out, what does it hurt?" Tepper said.

After Linda and Max had said their good-byes, Tepper brought the *Daily News* out of his carry-on bag and started to look through it. The front-page headline was ANOTHER CHORUS FROM BILL. The headline was superimposed on a nearly life-size picture of Bill Carmody, the Woodside Wacko, from the neck up. He was wearing a baseball cap decorated with the 4-H Club logo and the legend PIGS FOR KIDS—MORTON'S CORNER, IOWA. He appeared to be singing. Carmody had formally announced that he would be in the race for City Hall. In his announcement, he had not mentioned Frank Ducavelli by name, but he had said that the voters could count on Bill Carmody to be a servant of the public rather than the sort of authoritarian who would drive a lifelong New Yorker like Murray Tepper out of the city.

The *News* also carried a column by Ray Fannon. It talked about the dread of facing a mayoral campaign between the two candidates who had announced so far. "It's like standing out in the playground in sixth grade and suddenly realizing that the class bully is approaching you from one side and the class weirdo from the other," Fannon wrote. "All you can hope for is that the bell rings and recess ends before they arrive. In this case, though, after the bell rings one of them is going to be in charge of the city." There was a brief reference to the mayor's confrontation with Murray Tepper ("There is nothing more satisfying than seeing one of the quieter kids respond to the class bully's taunts by knocking him on his keister") but no mention of the theory that Murray Tepper might have engineered the entire affair.

"Well, I suppose we should get going," Tepper said to Ruth.

They stood and gathered up their carry-ons. "Do you want to stop at the newsstand and pick up the *Post* for the plane?" Ruth asked.

"The *Post*?"

"By the time we get there, it'll be afternoon," Ruth said. "In fact, in England, it's afternoon already."

"I hadn't thought of that," Tepper said. "By all means. Let's get the *Post*."

They stopped at the newsstand, and then headed for international departures.